the *Princess* and the CLOWN

IAN THOMAS MALONE

THE PRINCESS AND THE CLOWN by Ian Thomas Malone
Published by Green Muffin Publishing
Riverside, CT 06878
www.greenmuffinpublishing.com

ISBN-10: 0692727353
ISBN-13: 978-0692727355

Editor: Jessica Baumgartner
Cover Design: Wicked by Design
Formatting: Champagne Formats

Visit the author's website at IanThomasMalone.com

First Edition

Printed in the United States of America.

DEDICATION

For Henry James

CHAPTER
One

RALPH TOUCHET TOOK ONE MORE LONG DRAG OF HIS cigarette. He stomped it out on the ground and reached into his car's glove compartment.

"Fuck," he said, out loud as he grabbed the empty Altoid container. Time to go to work.

He checked his makeup in the side mirror and went around to the back of his truck to grab his bag. He let out a "shit," as he saw stray, playing cards throughout the old rucksack.

"Today might be the day I finally do it," he said to himself again.

Once the cards were organized, he hauled his bag toward the house where he'd be performing. A twin's birthday party should've meant more money, but the kids were different genders and the family told him they were bringing in a female performer as well, much to Ralph's chagrin. Clowns weren't supposed to be only appealing to little boys. Such a characterization could be crippling for Ralph's industry.

He took a few, deep breaths hoping that this would whisk away the cigarette smoke. He thought back to the 80s and 90s when people hardly cared how clowns behaved around children. He tried to remember the last time he'd packed a flask for a three hour "performance," while he squeaked his clown nose.

Calling it a performance kept him sane. Ralph could down a fifth of Jack and still be able to make balloon animals and talk in a stupid, fucking voice. That didn't take real talent. If only he hadn't been sacked from the circus.

"Motherfucker," Ralph said, as he walked up to the house, a new McMansion. He knew, in this area, it must have cost at least three million. There were going to be a lot of rich assholes inside. He thought about turning around but the allure of the paycheck kept him going.

Afternoon parties were the worst. The sun beat down extra bright as if it was taunting anyone who dared to conduct commerce outside. Ralph wanted to know just exactly what it was that prompted these people to book him for four o'clock on a Saturday as if the rest of their day was completely filled up.

He rang the doorbell.

"Just a minute," called a voice from inside the house. "Jesus," Ralph replied, in a muffled voice. He wiped sweat from his brow and took a look at his arm, thankful that it didn't have a streak of white on it. Water resistant makeup was a godsend in Southern California.

The door opened.

"Hi, you must be Jango," said a blonde trophy wife in

THE PRINCESS AND THE CLOWN

yoga leggings. Ralph popped wood right in front of her, thankful that his baggy, polka dot, clown pants covered the boner.

"Yes ma'am. Jango the Clown, the finest clown on the West Coast, at your service." He extended his hand, which the woman took reluctantly.

"I thought the e-mail said to go around the back," she replied. "Oh. You're right. Yea. Sorry about that. Was thinking too much about the work, you know? My secretary must have forgotten to remind me." Lies.

The woman took a step back. "It's no trouble, why don't you head back around there now. Princess Aurora is already there. We just don't want the children to know you're here yet."

Fucking bitch, I've got to take a leak, thought Ralph to himself.

"Got it," he said, wishing he'd brought his cigarettes with him. The woman smiled.

"Great, you're supposed to start in half an hour. Please stay out of sight of the back patio until we're ready. My name is Hillary by the way." She shut the door before Ralph could respond, leaving him to wonder if she knew what a walking stereotype she was.

Ralph trudged across the lawn, taking a minute to peer in through a window at the party. Rich people with their privileged children filled the living room as they celebrated the birthday of some little shit. His lips salivated at the thought of the rum and cola he planned to drink later.

His partner for the day was seated at a table in one corner of the backyard. He took a brief look at the gated swimming pool, complete with water slide and diving board, before his eyes fixated on the princess before him. Ralph's hidden erection returned.

"Exiled out here too," he said, as he approached his fellow birthday party performer. She looked to be in her mid-forties, a bit old to be wearing a pink dress with layers of petticoats and a large, pointy hat. He could tell that the dress was of high quality and cost at least a couple hundred bucks.

"Princess Aurora" had dyed, blonde hair and a face that had been clearly, heavily augmented with makeup. Female performers in his field tended to vary quite a bit more in their appearance than the males, who could get away with their disheveled looks in baggy, clown clothes. It took guts for a woman not far from menopause to don an outfit like that.

"Exiled? Hardly," she replied, with a raspy voice. "They gave me a bottle of the bubbly water. Want a sip?"

"Nah I'm good," Ralph paused and answered, "That shit gives me gas and later, the runs."

"Charming," the princess said. "I'm Jules Hightower."

"Ralph." He looked down at his bag and spotted an old pack of American Spirits he'd stolen off a college kid at a frat party. "Care for a smoke?"

"What? Are you kidding?" she replied. "You'll get us both canned. Get yourself together you fucking clown and fix your hair."

Ralph noticed that his clown wig didn't feel right. He took out his pocket mirror to check. "Thanks." He paused, taking another look at her figure. "What do you eat to maintain a body like that?"

"Spanx and it's none of your fucking business you pervert. Don't you know where we are?"

"Ain't no one out here but us, princess," Ralph replied, rolling his eyes.

"If that's how you really feel, don't suppose you would object to going down on me, would you clown?" she said, taking another sip of her bubbly water.

Ralph paused to make sure he'd heard her right.

"Come again," he said.

"That's a bit presumptuous, but I would hope so," she replied. "Get down here before it passes."

Ralph wondered what "it" could be. He looked toward the house. The woman, Hillary, said the party wouldn't start for half an hour. *Was it worth the risk? What if they got caught and the payday was lost? Did it matter?* He didn't think so. *Even if someone did walk out, what were they going to do? Call the police and ruin the whole party?* Ralph knew he was in the clear.

He looked at the princess before him again, unsure if this was something he wanted to do with a complete stranger. He moved toward her and started to get down on his knees.

"Wait a second," he said. "What do I get out of this?"

She bent over in her chair and looked him right in the eye.

"Damned fool. No wonder you're a clown." She smacked him on the head before pulling up her skirts and said, "Now get in there and lick me."

Ralph let the tulle block out the world as he found

himself encapsulated by the insides of Princess Aurora. He reached his hands up, looking for her panties to pull down. His hands found her stocking garter straps.

"I'm not wearing any undies, get to work already. I feel a hot flash coming on," she said.

"That's a bit risky. You know how expensive this dress is? Why risk stains?" Ralph replied. He yelled out as she crushed his head with her knees.

"Shut up. I don't want to know why you know that you sick fuck."

She was moist. Ralph enjoyed himself as he did his business on this sexually, explicit princess. He licked and he licked like Pooh enjoying some honey. He licked some more, until there was no more. Then he licked until he found some more savory juices.

The nectar filled his mouth with the tangy sensation of an expired carton of half and half he might find in the back of his fridge. Tempting yet forbidden, until the moment comes where wrong becomes right. He felt a mild squirt in his trousers as he thought about using Jules' juices in a White Russian, paired perfectly with the vodka and Kahlua.

The princess moaned like she was in the middle of a *Keeping Up with the Kardashians* marathon. Her ecstasy sounded like she'd just won a year's supply of chicken sandwiches from Chick Fil A.

"Oh clown," she said. "I'd allow you to jest in my court any day." Ralph almost gagged on a mixture of his fluids and hers.

He continued satisfying her royal highness for a few

more minutes until he felt another blow to his head.

"Cut that out will you, it's bad enough down here in this dark, hot space," he said, as she kneed him one more time.

"Is it almost time to begin Mr. Hunter?" Jules asked, as she shifted her petticoats to allow Ralph to get a breath of fresh air. A banner across the table shielded their lewd act from their employer. He coughed as he found himself on the ground of the well-tended lawn, which didn't appear to comply with California's drought initiative.

"Yes, almost," said Mr. Hunter, who paused before adding, "My wife told me Jango had arrived. Do you know where he is?" Ralph coughed and stood up.

"Here I am. Dropped my mirror. Wanted to reapply my face once more because of the heat. This weather is giving the water resistant stuff a run for its money."

He stared at his employer, hoping that he'd made the story at least somewhat believable. He tasted Jules on his lips. Her nectar reminded him of a gas station Slurpee, only it didn't cost eighty cents.

Mr. Hunter looked at him for a second. "Right. Of course. Very good. Ten minutes or so. Figure we'll introduce you together and then Jango can take the boys over there past the pool. Can I get you a bottled water or anything?"

A smile grew across Ralph's face as he thought about all the things he'd like to ask for right about now. A beer. A marijuana cigarette. Use of the master bedroom.

"A bottled water sounds nice sir." Mr. Hunter nodded and took his leave.

"Nice recovery," Jules said, as she stood up to straighten her dress.

"Recovery," Ralph laughed. "Please. That man didn't have a fucking clue what was going on."

He opened his mirror to assess the damage to his face. There were some spots around his mouth and his lipstick needed touching up.

"How about that," he said. "Didn't all melt off in your pussy's inferno."

Jules rolled her eyes. "Charming once again. You sure do know how to talk to a lady." Apparently not shaken by his flirtatious shortcomings, she sat back down and asked, "So. How long have you been in the business?"

Ralph dusted a sheet in his makeup and began reapplying it to the messed up areas.

"The business? I've been clowning since I was seventeen. Children's birthday parties are just a side job until I make it back to the big show."

"A side job," she said, doing little to hide her condescension. "So you perform with a company then? Or you've got some other high paying clown job?"

Ralph wanted to yell, but paused for a second to breathe. He remembered the anger management course his ex-wife Sandra had made him take before she ended up leaving him anyway.

"Not at the moment. I've had my share of carnival action."

"I see. So was it drugs or alcohol that derailed the Jango express? Maybe a mixture of both." This woman was starting to get on his nerves.

"Look lady, I don't see what high horse you think you have a right to sit on making fun of how I earn a living. You think I like performing for a bunch of snot nosed, little shits? I do what I need to do to survive. It ain't like you're some god-damned queen."

She pulled a flask out of her purse and took a sip.

"Want some?" she asked.

Ralph laughed. "I don't drink on the job much anymore. How'd you even get hired anyway?"

"You were close clown. You're right. I ain't some god-damned queen. I'm a motherfucking princess. Don't you ever forget it, not for a second. You hear me? I own you for as long as I damn well please."

Ralph popped wood yet again. The last time he'd had this many erections in such a short span was when he'd found a Jane Fonda aerobics tape at Goodwill. His member pulsated at the thought of leotard wedgies.

He saw a woman with a water bottle approaching them. He pointed over his shoulder to tell Jules to put away the flask.

"Here you go Mr. Jango. Mr. Hunter told me to inform you that the party will be starting soon. The helium tank is all set up at your table. Please let me know if there's anything else you need."

Ralph picked up his bag. Looking at the princess one more time, he turned to the woman and said, "Thanks. I've got everything I need."

CHAPTER
Two

I T ONLY TOOK FOUR SECONDS INTO HIS JUGGLING ACT FOR Ralph to remember why he chose this profession. It didn't matter that he was twenty pounds overweight. It all looked like stuffing under his baggy pants. His grimy skin, marred by acne and withered with years of tobacco abuse couldn't be seen under his white palette.

Ralph was a loser. Jango was a star. Little kids looked up to the man who could keep four balls moving through the air without any trouble at all. Ralph's daughter didn't even return his calls.

He missed the days at the circus. Performing with a troupe, especially his old partner Fuzzy, really brought out the smiles on people's faces. It made it all worth it, even when he was packed in a tiny car with a bunch of disgusting shits who hadn't showered in days.

"Who's ready for balloons?" he said, once he'd finished his juggling act. The kids all screamed liked they didn't know that the inflated bits of rubber would break in about two seconds. A line formed at his table.

He saw who he recognized as the birthday boy at the front. Walter, Willie, or something with a W.

"And what animal would the birthday boy like to have?" he asked in his over exaggerated, clown voice. The boy said nothing.

"Come on, Wyatt, pick something," a little shit said, behind him. Apparently, completely oblivious as to whose party it was. Ralph kept his thoughts to himself.

"Umm," Wyatt said. "Umm. Umm. A narwhal."

A narwhal. Ralph would've preferred just about any other water creature, but he said nothing as he picked out a blue balloon and put it on the nozzle at the top of the helium tank.

"One narwhal, coming right up."

His hands moved like magic as he molded the balloon to fit the shape. He created what he knew to be a dolphin, only with an exaggerated horn created by maneuvering the front nose a bit. Wyatt smiled with glee as Ralph handed the boy his prize.

"That's incredible," Mr. Hunter said, as Wyatt ran off with the narwhal. "How'd you do that?"

Ralph smiled and said, "These magic hands can do many things."

Ralph hated balloons. He knew he could tie just about anything but the sentiment associated with them always brought him down. Balloons reminded him of Natalie, his daughter.

He thought back to his days at the circus when Sandra would bring her by before a show so she could watch her father transform into Jango. The way she'd laugh whenever he'd make funny noises as she squeezed his nose. To anyone else, it might seem like trivial memories but those were the moments Ralph missed when he looked back on the days gone by.

Next up were some card tricks that almost put Ralph to sleep. *YouTube* had sucked all the fun out of that kind of magic. Nowadays, any punk could put up a "tell all" video and Ralph's entire repertoire could become dated to any audience who knew how to use a computer. Fortunately, these little kids could appreciate the skill in his craft.

He looked over the pool toward the girls' entertainment. He closed his eyes just for a second to imagine the words coming out of Jules' mouth as if they were directed only at him. This fantasy caused him to imagine other places he'd like to find Jules' mouth.

After his show, it was time for cake. The two groups reconvened, leaving Ralph to himself while he put away his belongings. Out of the corner of his eye, he saw a woman in pink approaching him.

"I've never been one for modesty clown but I think you got the louder applause. What does that say about me?" Ralph didn't know how to address the suddenly reasonable princess.

"Boys scream louder. What's the toughest balloon animal you had to make?" asked Ralph. She put her hand to her chin as she thought about the answer. Ralph admired her pink, satin gloves, which protected her from the germs that were all too common at these sorts of parties.

"Some girl wanted a snowman, like from that movie.

So I took a white balloon and made a human. Tried to. Thing just came out looking like a disfigured dwarf. You?"

"Nothing's difficult for me anymore," Ralph said, overcome with a sudden rush of confidence.

"That's good to know," said Jules, who put her lips to her purse and leaned her head back. Ralph wanted to point out that her attempts to conceal her drinking were fooling no one, but opted not to. *She can drink if she wants to*, he thought to himself.

Mr. Hunter came back over once the cake was finished. "Thanks for putting on a great show, you both did a great job." He handed Jules her check first. As he handed Ralph his, he leaned in and whispered, "I put in a little something extra. My mind is still blown from that fucking narwhal. You're a genius."

Ralph couldn't help but hate Mr. Hunter as he took the money. He appreciated how the man showed his gratitude in a tangible fashion that a bartender would accept later on in the evening, but part of Ralph loathed the idea of tipping a clown. *The money was meaningless to a man like Mr. Hunter so what did it matter?* Ralph tried to stop himself from thinking about it any longer. Not with Jules right there beside him.

"What was he whispering about?" Jules asked, as Mr. Hunter walked away. Ralph felt a bit taken aback, by her nosiness.

"Never you mind what he gave me woman. Who do you think you are asking a man about something that was clearly meant to be private?"

"I think I'm someone you're going to buy a drink for."

She folded her check and put it into her purse.

Ralph couldn't believe this woman's nerve. "Are you going to make it worth my while if I do?" he asked, not caring how that might be perceived. He didn't view her as a classy woman, but rather as someone who got off on men telling her their intentions.

"Maybe. Just maybe. Only if you're a good clown."

As they walked away from the party, Ralph removed his clown wig. He waved it in the air a few times in a desperate attempt to clear the stink his balding head had left inside. It'd been at least five years since he'd washed the thing. The rubber never held its form after a rinse.

"Where's your car?" he asked, as he noticed her following him to his truck.

"I took an Uber here," she replied.

"Uber? In that outfit? Do you get off on shocking every fucking person you meet?"

"Yea. That's me all right. I sucked the driver off all the way here. Only gave him three stars though."

Ralph tossed his bag in the back of his truck. "You're one strange woman, you know that." She stopped in front of the car.

"You really think I blew the driver?"

"What am I supposed to think? I ate you out, what, an hour ago? How is that any different?"

She pulled a pack of cigarettes out of her purse. She took her gloves off, causing Ralph to stop and admire her perfectly, manicured hands.

He nodded toward the pack and she tossed him a cigarette.

"I got my license taken away after my third DUI. Ran over a mailbox and into an above ground pool. Flooded my fucking engine."

"Jesus," Ralph said, as he smoked the cigarette. "You at least perform for the family?"

"Fuck, no. That was in Florida. I owe them a couple grand for the damages and all, but they're not going to see a dime of that with me out here. Serves them fucking right for not putting the pool in a fucking hole where it belongs," she replied, as she climbed into the passenger seat.

Ralph coughed as he thought about holes. "You're a real piece of work, you know that princess?" He took off his clown shirt and put a white t-shirt on. He looked at the houses for peeping eyes, and removed the belt on his pants.

"Atta boy Jango. Let's have a look at that trouser snake of yours." Her voice carried.

"Will you shut the fuck up? I'm changing in broad daylight and you're talking about whipping out penises and shit. You got a filter on that mouth of yours hotcakes?"

"Oooh. Hotcakes. That's the kind of talk that can really get a girl wet. Oh clown, don't stop baby. Your words alone can induce moisture in my south pole."

Ralph stopped for a second to consider what he was getting himself into. She reminded him of his ex-wife. Knew exactly what to say to get him to do what she wanted. He wondered if that could also be what he wanted. A strong, authoritative woman.

He put on a pair of jeans and took the belt from his clown pants. Jules watched him put them on without saying anything, which made him feel self-conscious. "What?"

he asked.

"What do you mean what? Did I say something ass-hole?" Ralph stared at the ground as he blew a puff of smoke out through his nostrils.

"You looked like you had a snide remark waiting to crawl off the tip of your tongue. Well, go on, out with it."

She put her feet up on the dashboard, causing her skirts to take up most of the space in the truck.

"If I had something to say about watching you squeeze your fat ass into those jeans, believe me, you'd be the first to know."

Charming. Part of Ralph wanted to kick her straight to the curb. Instead, he climbed into the truck and turned the ignition on.

CHAPTER
Three

They arrived at The Brimstone Saloon, a local dive in West Compton. Ralph would have never thought to take a woman there, but Jules struck him as an exception. The place smelled like an old dumpster filled with corpses marinating in stale beer. Any woman who would even think to ask to be eaten out at a children's birthday party would fit in well with the ambiance.

"What a lovely place you've taken me to," she said. "You can leave if you don't like it. I ain't going to some fancy place where drinks cost ten bucks for the likes of you."

"Oh please. As if you'd ever be let into to one of those places. They'd take one whiff of you and send you right back out the door." Jules laughed.

Ralph started to grow tired of Jules' mean spirited comments.

"Look, you're the one freeloading off my truck and, presumably, my paycheck. If you've got something that's genuinely fucking funny to say, have at it. Comments about my appearance and my smell, or lack thereof, don't belong in this bar. You hear me?"

She gave him a look of disgust.

"Why don't you get me a seven and seven?" She hiked up her dress as she went to find a seat, like some alcoholic Cinderella prancing around at the ball.

Ralph thought about going into the bathroom to wash off his makeup, but instead he headed to the bar. Jules clearly didn't care about his appearance and he didn't particularly care if she did. The more he looked at her, the less she looked like the desirable goddess he'd first decided to eat out. Just a prima donna looking for a few free drinks.

He waved at Jeffrey, the owner, as he walked up to the bar.

"Good Lord, Ralphy, who's the broad in the getup?" Ralph didn't turn back to look at Jules, afraid that she'd enjoy the attention.

"Fucking psycho from the party I just performed at." Without thinking, he added, "Get a load of this. She told me to eat her out less than five minutes after I met her."

Manuel, a frequent patron of the bar and a fellow clown, leaned over from his stool and said, "That must have made you pause to think back to the old days. Fucking children's birthday party. What's this world coming to?"

Ralph suddenly felt dirty. "Don't say it like that. The kids were all inside. There was no one in the backyard but us."

"So you did?" asked Jeffrey, smiling like he already knew the answer.

"Yea. What was I supposed to do? It ain't exactly every

day that a woman asks you for sexual favors."

Manuel looked concerned. "Did you check for bumps while you were down there?"

Ralph groaned. "Bumps. What the fuck are you talking about?"

"Bumps," Jeffrey said. "You know, herpes." Ralph slammed his hand on the bar counter.

"No, I had no fucking idea what you meant." He tried to keep his voice down so Jules wouldn't come over. "Thank God, I've got you two to keep me informed of this bullshit. Now get me a Pabst and a seven and seven and I ain't paying for either. That's what you get for making me think about that stuff."

He took the drinks and went back to the booth where Jules was sitting. She looked annoyed. "Here you go. What's with the pissed off face? I got these for free so we can have another round afterwards, on me. Ain't that lovely?"

"What kind of place is this?" She continued to look displeased as she took her first sip.

"What do you mean?" He thought they'd been over that already.

"I mean, I've been sitting here for close to ten minutes while you took forever getting our drinks and no one has come up to try to hit on me. Is this place filled with queers or something? A bunch of guys afraid to take a clown's woman away from him?" She gave him another dirty look, with her top teeth biting her lip.

Ralph took a sip of his beer to keep himself from laughing.

"Good God, when does this ridiculous bullshit end?

My woman. How about no one in here would think to hit on a girl in a princess costume who came in with a clown? No one who didn't want to get involved with some fucked up shit later."

"Fucked up shit, eh? I like the sound of that." She bit the tiny straw in her drink. Ralph sighed as he realized that the ridiculous bullshit was not going to end anytime soon.

They finished their drinks and Ralph went to get another round. When he came back and sat down, he asked, "So Jules, or rather, Princess Aurora. How long have you been performing?"

She snatched the drink like the question was some personal insult.

"Performing? You mean making balloon shapes and painting little kid's faces? Ten years, give or take. None of that fancy pro clown shit you used to do."

"I didn't used to. I'm in between jobs. At least I got a taste of the big leagues," he replied, defensively.

"Major league clowning. That sounds like a real high rolling job," she smiled, as she taunted him.

Ralph started to pick up on her game. "You're all talk, you know that," he said. "Am I?" she replied, biting down on her tiny straw again. Ralph noticed her bleached white teeth for the first time.

"Yea. You act like you're some queen, pardon, princess, of the universe but you're not. I mean look at you. Wearing that dress in here talking to a man in plain clothes with clown makeup on."

He stopped for a second before adding, "I know what you want. It's that drink. Now you've got it and now what?

I know. You want the dick, don't you?"

Her lips puckered. "Oh Jango, you've got me all figured out. Booze and boners are all I live for. Why don't we go back to your place and I'll show you what I really want?"

Ralph didn't entirely like the sound of that. She could be some burglar waiting for a location to text to her boyfriend. Or a murderer.

Ralph wanted to feel more afraid by that thought than he actually did. Getting murdered wouldn't be the worst thing in the world. He took a look around the bar as he thought about who might miss him. He only needed one hand to count the people who might attend his funeral outside of those currently located in the Brimstone Saloon.

One possibility did sound unmistakably good. Sex. He thought about how badly he wanted sex compared to how much he cared about being killed. Getting robbed wouldn't be a big deal. He lived in a trailer and had nothing of value save for his clown gear and his smartphone. His computer was all shot to shit from looking at too much porn.

"All right," he said. "We'll go back to my place. You pull any weird shit on the way and I'll drop you right at the curb. You can wait for Prince Charming, but I doubt you'll find him in this neighborhood."

"Maybe I have. Maybe he's a frog waiting for that one kiss. Do you feel slimy clown?" she grinned.

Ralph didn't answer. He stood up and dropped a couple of bucks on the table. He waved to Jeffrey and Manuel and headed for his truck, wondering if he was making the biggest mistake of his life.

CHAPTER
Four

THEY ARRIVED AT RALPH'S TRAILER. THE AGED MOBILE home could use a paint job, but it served as a reasonably decent place to live for a person with no money. Ralph swore as they walked past his patio chair, which was covered in bird shit.

He held the door open for her as they walked into his crowded living area. He waited for her to say something obnoxious but Jules was quiet as she looked around the place. The wait started to get to him.

"Go on. Say something. Criticize the décor. Anything."

She laughed. "Masochistic are we? I'll say this. It smells a lot better than I was expecting."

Ralph took the backhanded compliment in stride.

"Drink," he asked, reaching for the bottle by the sink.

"Vodka and whatever you've got to put in it," she replied. He poured a little flat, club soda into a glass and handed it to her. Seeing that he had no other choices of alcohol, he made the same for himself.

"How long have you lived here," she asked. "It doesn't look *that* messy, unless you're just the tidiest clown I've ever seen."

Ralph took a sip of his drink.

"About two years. Got my own apartment after my wife kicked me out, but that wasn't worth it. It helps to be able to pack up and leave when you need to."

Jules kicked off her shoes and took a seat on a chair opposite from Ralph. She put her stocking clad feet onto his lap and said, "rub." Ralph obliged.

Ralph never considered himself to be much of a foot guy, but the hooves resting on him were almost enough to cause some spontaneous squirting.

Her silky, thigh highs added to the sensation of caressing the bunion on her big toe. She moaned in delight as he worked on it with both hands, moving in a clockwork direction over the bony growth. After a minute, he switched up his technique, getting under toward her heel with his right hand while his left tickled the top.

She sipped her vodka and let out squeals of pleasure.

"Those magic hands clown. Oh. Don't stop. Ever."

He thought back to his work with the balloon animals. That man, Mr. Hunter, paid him extra for being able to craft that fucking narwhal. Now, here he was, using his talents to give someone another form of pleasure.

He worked the bunion for a few more minutes. When it looked like Jules was about to pass out from delight, he stopped. She looked at him and downed the rest of her drink.

"Do you want to go to the bedroom," he asked.

"Wait," she said, as Ralph stood up. "Help me get out of my dress. I'm not going to have this thing dry cleaned for a quick fuck."

Ralph pretended not to hear the "quick fuck" comment as he unzipped the back of her princess costume. She pushed him back on his chair as she reached for another cigarette. From a seated angle, Ralph was treated to a full view of his goddess, his princess.

His erection returned as he saw a glimpse of her muffin top protruding from her shape wear as she stood before him, like Hera about to claim her prize of an innocent, Greek merchant. A push up bra protected her breasts that sagged with the stress of living in twenty-first century America.

"Don't cream yourself there clown. Get up." "Let me wash the makeup off," he replied, standing up. As he turned, she grabbed him.

"No. Leave it. I like you better with it on." He obliged.

As he opened the door, she pushed him onto the bed and mounted him. "Who's been a bad clown today?"

Ralph paused. "You. I'm the one who got paid extra, remember." Smack. She slapped him across the face.

"You're going to pay for that. Now worship me."

He turned her over off to the side of his slightly cramped, full-sized bed. He stuck out his tongue and waved it for her to see but he didn't immediately proceed to her private parts. Instead, he began to make his way up along the side of body.

His tongue found a crevice created by a large, stretch mark. His tongue explored the crater like he was trying to get the last bit of pudding out of the cup. He pulled off her shape wear, which caused a seemingly, insurmountable roadblock like the packaging from a technology product at Radio Shack. He was never going to get her open.

"Fucking amateur hour," she said, as she kicked up and pulled it off. She stuck her feet in his face and pushed on him as she pulled her undergarments off. Ralph imagined himself licking sausage out of its casing, while his own sausage tingled with glee.

Finally, after what seemed longer than the final two minutes of a professional football game, he reached the clitoris. He enjoyed being back in this familiar space, especially in a setting that was not as hot as the nine circles of hell Dante went through in his inferno, which couldn't have been much worse than a child's birthday party.

He licked for a good five minutes before he remembered something Manuel had said back at the pub. He came up for air and looked at Jules, who couldn't have looked more displeased with his resurfacing. She scoffed and grabbed a pillow.

"What are you doing? I didn't remember telling you I was done." Ralph tried to think of the right wording for what he wanted to say. "Well," she added. "Pussy got your tongue?"

"You're clean right?" She threw the pillow at him. "Excuse me. Clean? What kind of woman do you think I am?" He didn't know how to respond.

"It's a fair question. I like you, but I'm not about to catch something that causes my anus to bleed just because you participated in a gangbang at a McDonald's play place.

If you've got nothing to hide, why don't you just say it?"

She sighed. "I had crabs once ten years ago. Haven't felt an itch that wasn't caused by drugstore pantyhose in quite some time. You?"

Ralph appreciated her honesty. "I got the clap in clown school, but so did everyone else." Jules looked like she was about to say something, but paused.

"All right, now that story time is over, back to work. Am I clean? What a fucking idiot." She pushed his head down toward the bed with her foot and he resumed performing cunnilingus. He looked for bumps with his tongue, thankfully failing to identify any herpes-like bumps.

He started to think about his odd day while he went down on her. It'd been over a year since he last performed at a birthday party with another entertainer there. Doing separate shows was incredibly rare since few cared to spend that much money. It also usually meant that neither one of them would have any reason to interact with each other.

Yet, the two of them did. Almost immediately after meeting her, he found himself performing the same act he found himself occupied with now. He tried to imagine any other time where deja vu would involve eating a woman out. He couldn't even remember a time he'd eaten someone out, including his ex-wife, more than once in a single day. Sandra preferred his tongue in her back door.

After what must have been an hour, he felt juices splashing inside his mouth, like a faulty water fountain that suddenly came back to life. All his work had left him feeling dehydrated and her juices were more invigorating than even the finest sports drink. He stopped for a second to appreciate the flavor, expecting to go for more when he felt her pull away.

"All right, clown, you've been better than I expected. Now go fetch me one of my gloves." He started to climb off the bed before stopping, wondering what the hell she wanted her glove for.

"Why?" he asked. She sat up in the bed against the wall. "It's your turn silly. I'm not going to give you a rub and tug barehanded. What kind of lady do you think I am?"

A rub and tug? Ralph had taken a lot of shit from this woman today, but a line needed to be drawn somewhere.

"I don't think so," he said.

"What? You don't want me to give you a fairytale ending?" She had a grin on her face that gave away the fact that she expected him to be displeased.

"Oh, I want a fairytale ending. A hand job isn't going to cut it." Jules let out a cackle.

"Cut it?" Ralph knew this could be murky territory. Normal people didn't exactly respond well to demands for sex.

"Okay," he said. "If you think that a hand job is a fair way to reward all the pleasure I've given you over the course of this day, fine. You can be on your way."

Her jaw almost dropped, lingering in midair like a Starbucks customer who received the wrong order. "What are you talking about?"

He stopped himself from laughing. "You don't want to have sex? That's perfectly fine by me, but I don't want to have my junk fondled by some glove wearing prima donna when I could do a better job myself. I can call you a cab if you'd like. I don't feel like driving you home."

Instead of feeling like a selfish fool, Ralph smiled. He'd started to figure out what made Jules tick. Sex didn't turn her on; she got off on the power struggle. Wanking him would likely give her more satisfaction than sex ever could, knowing that she'd gotten him to listen to her every command. Once he made it clear that he wasn't going to play by those rules, the game changed.

"I see what you're up to clown. Well, I'm already soaking wet. It'd be a shame to waste my naturally lubed up pussy. It'd be a different story if I'd had to use any more of that lotion from the eye doctor." She grabbed him and pulled him back toward the bed.

Ralph fell backward onto the mattress. Crack. "Fuck," he said. Jules hovered over him.

"Finished already? What a pity."

Ralph moaned with pain. "No. My back. Fucking shit fuck. I'm okay."

"Are you," she whispered, leaning towards his face.

The smell of vodka and cigarette on her breath was the finest aphrodisiac he'd ever inhaled, even better than the inside of a Big Mac container that had been sitting out in the sun for a few days.

"Yea. I'm just not sure I can get hard right now. Back is all out of whack."

Ralph grew concerned that there could be another issue at play. Erectile dysfunction. A common enough ailment for middle-aged men and one that Ralph didn't usually have to deal with. The problem generally isn't a big problem when one is masturbating.

Between the back pain and the lack of ability to properly pop wood, Ralph was sad. He needed a clown of his own to cheer him up. He turned his head to look in the opposite direction as Jules, embarrassed with himself.

"Hang on," she said. "I have just what you need." Ralph didn't want to think about what that might be.

She left the bedroom for a few minutes and returned holding a bottle.

"Whoa," said Ralph. "I did a little blow and plenty of grass in my day, but pills aren't really my thing."

She opened the bottle and took one out.

"It's just Viagra," she said. "I pinched this bottle from a party I did a couple months ago. The master bathroom was stocked. Xanax, Vicodin, Oxy, and just about anything you'd need for a good time."

Ralph took the pill and swallowed. *What now?* He sat up in bed while he stared at his junk.

"It's not instantaneous," Jules said. "But maybe this will do the trick." She took off her bra.

Jules' breasts were a thing of beauty. They sagged, like the economy after the subprime mortgage crisis. Her shoulders followed in a similar downward motion like Atlas, angry that his name was used in the title of that Ayn Rand novel.

Ralph found his blood flowing, though he knew the Viagra would take at least a half hour to kick in. His purple helmet warrior sprung to duty as if General Patton had personally requested its service.

"All right princess, I think I'm hard enough," he said.

"Hard enough you say?" She moved toward him. "Normally, I'd make you get on top," she added. "But with your back the way it is, I think I can ride the clown car this time."

Ralph didn't appreciate the clown pun but he was thankful that she didn't try to make him pull a muscle. She climbed on top of him and grabbed his member with her hand. His body relaxed as he felt her touch, but only for a second.

"Wait. Don't we need a rubber?" He already had one kid he never saw. He didn't need another.

"How very proactive of you," she said, in a highly sarcastic tone. "I can't get pregnant anymore. You go to certain places too many times after doing certain activities and well, you probably don't need to know."

He tried to zone her out as he worked to keep his third leg stiff.

"You ready clown?" she asked. He nodded as the two let their powers combine.

Jules was an animal. She moved one-way and then another. She went hard for a while, until she switched gears to go slow.

Ralph moaned and groaned. He said, "Oh yea," followed by "damn that's good." He knew it was true. Jules knew her way around a mattress.

Normally, when he was at his computer wanking, he could only imagine what a woman's touch felt like.

Here, he had a woman right on top of him. Being inside her was almost an afterthought.

The bed squeaked as the two moved in relative unison. It sounded like a symphony of mice, lamenting the loss of a loved one to a fateful trap. The motion of the bed reminded him of a mall massage chair, except this one didn't cost three thousand dollars to take home.

He wondered how long he could keep going. The Viagra had to have kicked in by now, for he no longer worried about staying hard. Becoming as soft as a scoop of coffee bean ice cream didn't strike Ralph as a likely possibility.

She slapped him.

"Who's your princess?" she asked in a commanding voice. "Tell me. Yell my name bitch. I fucking own you, Jango."

He obliged. "Jules," he called out.

"More," she said.

"Jules," he replied, louder than before.

"Say it with my title." She slapped his stomach, which was drenched with sweat, causing her hand to make the sound a damp towel makes when it's dropped to the floor by an elderly man who's been in the sauna for too long.

"Princess Jules," he screamed, and exploded. She moaned with delight. He could feel sweat dripping down his sweat resistant makeup.

All of a sudden, he felt an explosion erupt from inside of him like he'd just eaten a Denny's breakfast combo. Though he was still hard, the fun was over. Jules hopped off and rolled over next to him.

"You were amazing," he said.

"I know," she replied. "You can sleep on the floor tonight." Before Ralph could respond, she pushed him off the bed.

CHAPTER
Five

OVER THE NEXT FEW DAYS, RALPH COULD ONLY THINK of one thing. Jules. Everything related back to her.

He sat at the bar of the Brimstone Pub, drinking an American lager, dreaming of his princess. He didn't notice that Manuel had been trying to get his attention. Manuel wouldn't look adorable in a pink dress nor would he ride him like the I.R.S. does with small businesses that make over two hundred fifty thousand dollars a year.

"Ralph, what the fuck is wrong with you?" Manuel said. "I'm trying to tell you something. Whatever. Guess I'll just keep the news to myself."

Ralph took a second to process what he'd only sort of heard.

"News," he said, his thoughts returning to Jules. The night they'd slept in relative proximity to each other had been one of the happiest of his life, though he paid for it the next morning when his back felt like he'd tried to carry four bags of groceries into his trailer at once.

"Yea," Manuel replied. "News. You know those reality television shows they make about people's jobs? The truck drivers and the lumberjacks."

Ralph didn't have a television, but he knew what Manuel was talking about. "Yea. I've heard of those."

"Right," Manuel said, who appeared dumbstruck by Ralph's dreamy demeanor. "So I get a call from Barnyard Paul, remember him?"

Ralph paused to think. "Yea. The rodeo clown down in Texas. What about him?"

Manuel sighed with apparent relief. "Okay good. Anyway, I get a call from Barn saying that he's been contacted by some producer looking to make a clown show. You follow?"

"I guess," a carefree Ralph replied. He thought Barnyard Paul was an asshole and especially hated how his preferred abbreviation was "Barn."

"All right, I'll stop talking. I can see you don't give two fucks about what I have to say."

Ralph could see that his friend was annoyed by his uninterested attitude.

"Nah Manuel, sorry. Can't stop thinking about the broad. Let me buy you another." He made eye contact with Jeffrey and put two fingers up. "Go on, buddy."

Manuel gulped down what was left in his gin and root beer.

"Okie dokes. Where was I? Right. So Barn gets the call about the show. Couple hours later, calls me. Asks if I know anyone who would be good in front of the camera for something like that."

Ralph waited for him to finish, not realizing that he already had.

"And?" he asked. "I told him I had a couple people in mind."

Ralph started to lose interest as Jeffrey brought over the drinks.

"Who were you thinking?" he asked, trying to think of the clowns he knew. Manuel only clowned part time. He gave up it full time in favor of a managerial position at Bed, Bath, & Beyond.

"I can't tell if you're being serious," he said. Ralph didn't respond. "You're going to make me spell it out dumbass. I was thinking about you."

Ralph tried to wander back to his daydream, unsure if he'd heard Manuel correctly. He didn't know how to respond.

"I haven't rodeo clowned since my late twenties you stupid shit. You know that."

Manuel looked like he'd smelled a bad fart. "Well, excuse me. Last time I ever try to do you a favor." He started to get off his chair.

"Look, I'm sorry, but you know that so why bother bringing it up?" Ralph didn't like getting his hopes up for things that could never pan out. He didn't know where Jules fit into that equation just yet, but he knew what the odds were.

"I know you still can, but it's not just about that. They're looking for all sorts of clowns. They want the best." Manuel talked in an upbeat tone like he actually believed this could go somewhere.

"If they want the best, why even bother?" said Ralph. "I'm past my prime Manuel. I'm all right doing the kid's shit, but TV? I mean really, who are we kidding here? Those days are over."

"Look man, it's no big deal if you're not interested." Manuel sighed, and gulped down the rest of his drink. "Thought I'd mention it. It's not for a couple weeks anyway. Think about it big guy. People still remember you. You don't need Fuzzy to mount a comeback." He patted Ralph on the back as he walked out of the bar.

Ralph felt a pang of despair creep up on him. He didn't know why he'd reacted in that way to Manuel's news. It didn't matter if he couldn't get on the show. He owed it to himself to at least try.

Another thought crossed his mind. Having a clown show on TV would renew people's interest in clowns. He might even start to book some more adult oriented gigs again. Being on the show would solidify his career, but it wasn't the end all be all. Texas presented many possibilities.

He thought about the last time he'd been on TV. Ralph and his partner Fuzzy used to perform tricks for a regional talk show way back when those were still on the air. The crowd had roared with applause, but that wasn't Ralph's fondest memory from the evening. He and Fuzzy had plowed through a quart of the host's finest single malt before running around tossing flaming rubber duckies at each other on live television.

Jeffrey came over to take Manuel's glass. "What were you two talking about?" he asked. "Clown business. But for real this time." Jeffrey laughed. "Clown business" was code for dirty topics when other people were in earshot.

"How's your woman?" Jeffrey asked. Ralph groaned and looked at his phone.

"Haven't heard from her in a few days. I guess maybe that's the way it was meant to be."

"You fucked her once," Jeffrey said, as he poured Ralph another beer. "That's more than most guys could ever say about a girl who prances around in a fairy costume."

"A princess costume," Ralph corrected him. "But, you're right, she was totally crazy. Best to have a one-and-done."

He sucked down the suds by himself, wondering if he actually meant what he said. He missed Jules. The smell of her hair, conditioner mixed with hairspray and cigarette. Her stretch mark that resembled the Rio Grande. The way she rode him like an old station wagon trying to make it up a hill.

He'd given her his card the morning after their night together when he drove her home. She rented a room on the second floor of an old woman's house in San Pasqual. Before she left, she promised she'd take him out to dinner one day in return for the ride, an invitation that seemed emptier and emptier as the days passed.

He tried to focus on the cricket match on the TV. Jeffrey only liked showing European sports, saying that American football didn't have enough action. His eyes kept focusing on his phone on the table.

He noticed a woman with rainbow hair at the other end of the bar watching him. He gave her a nod and she motioned for him to come over to her. Ralph almost ignored her, assuming she was referring to someone else until they made direct eye contact. Ralph couldn't believe he might have a chance at sex twice in one month as he walked over.

"Another for the lady," he said, to Jeffrey as he sat down. "The name's Ralph." He extended his hand. "Marshmallow," she replied. She took her drink from Jeffrey and clanked it against his glass. He barely even registered her strange name in his daze of disbelief.

"So Ralph," she said. "What do you do?"

Ralph opened his mouth to respond, but stopped himself. Clowns weren't exactly revered as sex symbols. "Entertainment," he replied. "You?"

"The service industry." She picked a Maraschino cherry out of her drink and bit into it. Ralph's ex was a waitress. This could work out well for him.

"Would you happen to be on the search for a good time this evening?" she asked, licking her top teeth with her tongue as she reached over to pat Ralph on his leg. Ralph started to stutter, doing his best to process this seemingly unrealistic proposition.

"Uh," he said, "I'm always on the hunt for a good time."

She bit down on her lower lip and moved her hand closer to his genital region.

"You got a place nearby?" she asked. Something didn't feel right about this encounter. It was too easy. The same could be said for Jules but she at least was also in the business. Clowns often fooled around with other clowns. Everyone knew that. So what was this woman's deal?

"Uh, yea," Ralph replied, unsure how he felt about this forward woman.

"What are we still doing here then?" Marshmallow in-

37

quired, as she slurped down the rest of her drink. Ralph banged on the counter with his knuckle, thinking that it would make a weird sound if he was dreaming. The counter sounded like normal.

He took a look around the bar at the rest of the patrons. The Brimstone clientele were mostly male, leaving Ralph to wonder one simple question. *Why him? What put Ralph apart from all the rest of the men Marshmallow could have with a simple stroke of the leg?*

"Okay," he said, pulling out a couple bills for Jeffrey. He gave the bartender a puzzled glance as he started to walk toward the exit with his newfound friend.

His eyes wandered to Marshmallow's oversized ass. It must have been that big when she came out of the womb for her mother to name her that. He tried to think of other girls with the name Marshmallow that he knew. A girl from middle school came to mind, until he remembered that her name was Maddy.

They got into his truck and drove back to Ralph's trailer. As they pulled up alongside it, she asked, "Is this your place?"

Ralph didn't normally feel self-conscious about his cramped living space, but something felt oddly firm in Marshmallow's tone, like she needed to be sure this was where he lived. He didn't know what it would matter if this was just the place he used to bang girls behind his wife's back. She hadn't asked enough questions to really be concerned about that.

"Sure is," he replied.

"Good." She paused and looked away from him, as if

she had more to say.

"Okay. It's going to be two hundred for two hours plus another twenty-five for the cab ride back. Is that cool with you?"

"What?" Ralph quickly replied. He had no clue what she was talking about. "Oh honey, you didn't think this was free did you?"

It all started to make sense.

I don't know what I was thinking," he said, his voice trembling.

"Did you really think I'd sleep with someone like you, just like that?" she asked.

"No. I guess not." Ralph quivered. He started to cry.

CHAPTER
Six

A FEW DAYS LATER, RALPH SMOKED A CIGARETTE ON HIS outdoor lounge chair, which was now free of bird droppings. He thought about Marshmallow and how stupid he'd been. She didn't look like a woman who was completely out of his league but those kinds of women didn't seduce middle-aged, overweight drunks in bars.

"You're not a drunk," he said, out loud to himself as he puffed away. "Not yet at least." A half consumed beer can at the side of his chair begged to differ.

He knew who to blame. Himself. Like most human beings, Ralph enjoyed sex. Being a relatively unattractive professional clown, he didn't find many places to put his penis besides his hand.

He thought about what he could do with the rest of his day. He had a party to perform at in two days, leaving him plenty of time to do the things that mattered most to him. Drink, smoke, and wank.

His phone vibrated in his pocket. He didn't recognize

the number. It could be a client, but it was probably a tele-marketer or one of those robocalls talking about preap-proved loans. Ralph didn't want to answer, but he decided that the worst thing that could happen was a little human interaction. Living in a trailer by yourself can get awfully lonely.

"Jango the Clown," he said, his customary greeting. He didn't have a separate line for business related inquiries.

"Jango," said a woman's voice. "I hear you perform many tricks with your tongue. I was hoping to book you for later this evening."

Jules. The princess had finally called, more than a week later. He thought back to the olden days before cell phones and remembered how common that used to be. Supposed-ly, intensified the desires.

"Hold on. Let me have my secretary check my sched-ule. Just a moment please." He moved the phone away from his ear as Jules shouted expletives into the phone.

"Tonight works. Where is the party happening?" His mildly successful attempts at keeping the flirtatious ex-change going came to an end when Jules said, "You can pick me up at seven-thirty." She hung up before he had a chance to respond.

Ralph took one last drag of his cigarette and stomped it out on the floor. He smiled. He had a date tonight.

One problem presented itself. *What to wear?* His knees creaked as he stood up from his chair and headed into his trailer to examine his wardrobe.

His favorite dress shirt, a green short sleeved, button down from T.J. Maxx, had a cigarette burn in it. He'd thrown out the blue one he bought the same day after puking on it one night. That left a plaid shirt from Target. It would have to do. Jules couldn't be too picky about appearances.

He tried it on to make sure it would fit. He had to suck his stomach in a bit but none of the buttons popped off as the fabric pressed against his gut. This would do just fine.

He grew anxious. He didn't need to pick her up for a few hours. Plenty of time to do something. *But what?*

Ralph grabbed his keys and headed from the Brimstone Saloon. This decision presented a bit of a risk if Marshmallow was there looking for clients. Bad karma. He couldn't stay away from there forever.

He tried to limit himself to two beers, but a third became inevitable as he sucked down the suds during a heated debate with Jeffrey over the 1988 Summer Olympics. He belched as he drove along I-405. A cigarette kept his mind occupied as he made his way along the monotonous road.

Manuel and Jeffrey had pestered him as to why he'd worn a dress shirt, an infrequent wardrobe choice. Ralph kept his date to himself. After the Marshmallow debacle, he decided that what he got up to with women should be kept to himself.

He pulled up alongside Jules' house. A classy man might think to ring the front door. Ralph considered this before remembering that she only rented space on the top floor and may not want her roommate, or whatever you'd call the old hag, to know her personal business. Instead, he honked the horn of his truck.

The horn made a pathetic squeal. He knew he needed a new vehicle but this would have to do until he made a ton of money off that clown TV show. The thought of that actually working out made him laugh out loud. He honked one more time before he heard Jules scream back, "I heard you the first fucking time asshole." He smiled as he heard the sound of his Jules, his princess.

Jules came out through the front door. She wore jeans and a yellow t-shirt with the word, "haste" across it. Ralph shook his head as he realized he should have expected something like this. He wondered if he should have been the one to plan their evening.

She said nothing as she climbed into his truck.

"Shouldn't you have your own entrance or something? What about your privacy?" he asked, looking at the house.

"Ha. Privacy. Who can afford that? Where are you taking me? Hopefully somewhere with unlimited breadsticks," she cackled, as she lit the cigarette.

The muscles in his jaw tensed up as he fought to contain his nervousness. He had no answer.

"Hang on a second. You said you owed me a dinner and you were the one who called me. Tell me how that's fair?"

She blew smoke in his face. "Looks like chivalry really is dead. You expected a free meal from a woman you just met because you drove her home?"

Ralph didn't want to let this go. "Only if it's a meal that's been promised to me." He grabbed the cigarette out of her hands and began to smoke it himself.

"You know what? Fine. I had ulterior motives for calling you up anyway." Jules smirked.

Ralph shook his head. "Oh," he replied. "What might those be?"

She grabbed his crotch. "Drive clown. I'll tell you when we get to the restaurant."

Ralph didn't like where this was going, but he obliged and stepped on the gas. Neither spoke as they puffed on their cigarettes. Ralph especially enjoyed his as he tried to taste Jules on the filter. He gave it little licks with his tongue, hoping to get a taste of her nectar.

"You work any parties this week?" she asked, in an oddly, concerned fashion. Ralph started to think that Jules was the jealous type. Unless she seriously wanted something.

"I did a school function on Monday and I've got one on Friday," he said. The school year didn't call for many parties during the week, though libraries, churches, and schools often booked him for various functions. The pay wasn't great, but it was enough to keep food on the table and beer in his stomach. Even if the food consisted of Hot Pockets and Pop Tarts.

"Good, good," she replied. Ralph waited for her to continue, but she remained silent. This woman had something on her mind.

They kept driving for a little while longer. Ralph grew impatient, as he didn't know where they were going. Gas didn't grow on trees and he didn't relish the idea of lining some Saudi Arabian prince's pockets while his own princess picked out a restaurant.

"Do you know where we're even going?" he asked.

"Yeah," she replied. "Right there." She pointed at a Del Taco location.

"No," said Ralph. "We are not eating at Del Taco. This is not a restaurant" Jules scoffed at him. "Excuse me? What do you have against Tex-Mex? Are you some kind of racist white supremacist clown? Christ. That would explain that hideous wig you wore at the party."

Ralph chose not to respond as he pulled into the fast food "restaurant" parking lot.

"This doesn't count as my dinner," he said. "Sure it does," Jules replied. "Remember, I call all the shots. Be thankful you're even getting food out of this."

Ralph stomped his cigarette out on the floor. He supposed she had a point. *What fancy restaurant would take the two of them?* Even if they had a reservation, the maître d' was bound to come up with some excuse for why their table was suddenly unavailable.

He tried to hold Jules' hand as they walked up the building. She pulled away and slapped him. "Gross, nice try you pervert," she said. Ralph grinned, seeing the expected result right before his eyes.

They walked up to the counter. Jules ordered a bunch of tacos and burritos and walked away to take a seat. Ralph and the cashier stared at each for about thirty seconds. He looked at the register and handed the employee a twenty.

"Figures," he said.

He filled up their drinks and sat down at their table. "I knew you'd pay," she said. She took a sip of her drink and spit it out. "Water," she added, practically yelling.

"Yeah. I told him not to worry about your drink when you walked away. Hope, that's not a problem." She poured her water on the floor.

"Oh, come on now, that's just rude." She didn't appear to care as she walked up to the soda dispenser to refill her cup. "You're not supposed to do that," he called out. The cashier had disappeared as they were the only two customers.

"You're going to get us in trouble," Ralph said, as she returned to the table.

"I'm not even going to ask you if you think I give two shits," she replied. Ralph chose not to respond.

The cashier returned to the front of the restaurant carrying a tray with their food. Ralph stood up to retrieve it. Jules stuck her foot out in an attempt to trip him that failed, thankfully for Ralph.

Ralph returned with the food and an assortment of hot sauces.

"Bon appetite," he said as he bit into a taco. It wasn't fine dining, but it tasted quite delicious.

He watched Jules go to town on a huge burrito. "Damn, where do you put all that?" he asked, taking another stab at flirting.

Her eyes pierced his as she replied, "First my stomach, then my ass. You want to take a look?"

"Sure." Ralph snickered.

They ate in silence for a few minutes until Ralph remembered why they were there.

"You were going to ask me something," he said.

Jules continued to peruse her food selection. She'd ordered at least fifteen taco and burrito variations. A few times, she picked something up, opened it, and put it back, leaving Ralph to wonder why she'd even ordered it in the first place.

"Yes. What are you doing tomorrow?" Ralph shuddered as he wondered what she could possibly want him for.

"That depends," he said.

"All right, have it your way asshole. Stick up your nose at paid work." She tore into a new taco even though she hadn't finished the one she'd been eating.

"Paid work? Why does everything have to be so cryptic with you?" He liked Jules, but her antics wore thin on his frail psyche.

"I got asked to do a party tomorrow. Some parent saw my Yelp! page or something. I don't fucking know. Anyway, he asked me what I was good at so I told him."

"And," Ralph replied, unsure where he fit in to all of this. "Well, I'm not that good. This guy lives in Beverly Hills and said he'd pay me a grand to make his kid's day so I said I'd do it. What else was I supposed to do?"

Ralph paid close attention to her tone as she talked about the money. He'd done two parties in Beverly Hills over the past few years. Both paid more than that. Coupled with the increase in the cost of living and the elite's general desire to look out for the working class, Ralph knew Jules had been ripped off.

"A thousand you say," Ralph said. He watched Jules' eye pulsate. He wasn't the smartest man in the world, but even he could spot a lie when he saw one.

"Yea, pretty good isn't it?" Jules replied, keeping her eyes on her food. "I figured, since it's so much, we could go in on it together. I don't want to show the rich fuck's kid a bad time and let's face it. You're a better performer than I am."

Ralph took a sip of his drink to stifle his laughter. Jules spoke the truth, but her compliments were far from genuine. He started to see the situation she found herself in.

Odds were, Jules lied about her abilities to the parent. Over exaggerated her skill set to get the gig. She also couldn't drive, making Ralph valuable for another reason.

"What's the split?" he asked. He watched Jules' right hand twitch as she stumbled to think of a response. "Does sixty-forty work?" she replied. "Sure, sixty for me since I have the car and I'm the better performer."

Ralph waited for the real kicker. "That doesn't seem fair since I found the guy, but if that's what you want, fine." Bingo.

"That works," he began to say. "But I want sixty of the real commission." A bit of lettuce fell from Jules' mouth.

"Real commission?" Jules' usual confidence had all but vanished.

"Jules, I'm not stupid and I know a con when I see one. Maybe it's not completely your fault. It might have worked if you weren't so easy to figure out."

"Fuck you. I don't need your help." She pelted him with a pinch of beef.

He wiped the meat off his face. "Sure, you do. You just want to be paid more so you can maintain your sense of superiority. I get it. I've done parties out there. A grand is decent money, but it's not what those guys pay. Try doubling it, at least, if it's Beverly Hills these days, and on short notice during the week. Unless, you're just the worst negotiator I've ever seen."

Jules clapped her hands together. "Almost double asshole. Eighteen hundred. If you don't believe me, I'll show you the damn check after the party. But it's fifty/fifty. I don't care if you solved the mystery like you're goddamned Nancy Drew."

Ralph tried not to show how pleased he was with himself. "Deal." He bit into another taco.

They finished their meal, consuming a disgusting amount of calories and carbohydrates with only minimal nutrition. Once Ralph put down the wrapper of his last taco, he leaned his head back.

"Damn," he said. "I feel lethargic, like it's Thanksgiving dinner and I ate a whole tin of spam."

"I don't feel tired. I feel horny." Jules made slurping sounds with what was left of her beverage. "Horny," replied Ralph. "You're kidding."

She kicked him under the table. "You think I'd kid about that jackass? Now can you get hard without a pill or what?"

Ralph thought for a second. "Not right here. Ouch." She kicked him again.

"There's a bathroom dumbass." She stood up. "Well, come on."

Ralph grew erect as they walked to the bathroom. It had a toilet and a urinal, but the lock on the door indicated that it was typically only used by one person at a time.

"You need a tug or something?" Jules asked, looking right at him. Ralph shook his head as he processed what was happening.

"Do me from behind," she demanded. "I don't like looking at your face when you don't have your clown make-up on." Ralph felt self-conscious about his acne, but kept quiet. Bad skin wasn't keeping him from getting laid.

The bulge in his trousers indicated that he needed no Viagra this time.

"No tugs necessary, I'm all ready to go."

"Good." She pulled down her jeans and leaned against the bathroom wall. "Get to it then," she said, in her usual domineering voice.

Ralph stared at the back of Jules' luscious, dyed blonde hair for a little while. *Did he really want to do her from behind in a Del Taco bathroom?* Of course he did.

He grabbed his hardened member and placed it inside Jules, a soothing action like a soccer mom licking a soft serve nonfat Greek frozen yogurt.

"That's the spot," she said, moaning with the delight of a comic book geek at the premiere of a new Marvel movie.

Ralph tried to perfect his craft. He imagined Mr. Miyagi showing him the wax on/wax off technique as he waxed the insides of Jules with his own special sauce.

Ralph and Jules both expressed their pleasure in different fashions. Ralph sounded like a bear who had found an Olive Garden dumpster with its lid open. Jules' long drawn out moans resembled a junior in college reading *Infinite Jest* for the first time, seemingly endless, but unmistakably orgasmic every step of the way.

Jules reached her hand back and grabbed ahold of Ralph's love handles. She squeezed his blubber like a dessert chef gently crafting a blackberry mousse. Ralph's hands worked their way up from her buttocks, in search of his favorite stretch mark. The Rio Grande may be swimmable, but Jules had all the fluids he needed.

A knock on the door startled them.

"We're busy," Jules yelled, apparently oblivious to the fact that they were in what was labeled as the men's bathroom.

"How much longer," a voice replied, which could have belonged to the cashier.

"Double flusher," Ralph said, as he thrust into his princess.

"Gross man, do that somewhere else," the voice answered.

"Do you know where the fuck we are asshole? It's a fucking bathroom," Jules added. The voice behind the door did not respond.

Ralph couldn't believe his stamina. It had been at least seven minutes and he was still hard. Normally, it took him about three to finish in front of his computer because that was about as long as it took for the porn videos he watched to start buffering.

He heard a rumbling sound. He couldn't tell if it came from Jules or from him. He looked down at his tummy and felt an unmistakable quake throughout his body. A similar sound came from Jules.

"Hurry up," she said. "I don't feel so good." Ralph didn't feel so hot either.

"Give me a second," he said as he tried to adjust his position. "I'm losing it," he said.

"Do it Jango. Cum in your princess. Now," she said, and Ralph did as he was told, almost on autopilot. The blissful feeling that normally comes from climax only lasted for a second, as the stomach pains intensified, like the bridge of an EDM song.

"Shit," Jules said, as she pushed him away and sat on the toilet. "Get out," she screamed. Ralph's stomach had different plans.

"I can't. I have to go too," he replied, squatting and bringing his knees together, hoping that would serve as some magical cure. It didn't.

"Damn it Ralph," Jules said, as she started to defecate. "Go in the other bathroom."

Ralph turned and spotted the urinal. "I'm not going to make it," he said, and turned to the urinal to make alternative arrangements. His trousers lay at his feet as he shuffled toward his solution.

"No, Ralph, no," Jules said. The sound of diarrhea trickled from her anus like a slow drip coffeemaker, producing similarly colored fluid.

"I'm sorry," he replied, as he squatted into the urinal, producing foul smelling chunks of his own beef stew. The bathroom smelled like the Grim Reaper after he'd taken a CrossFit class.

One emotion made its way through the smog created by the smell of concurrent anal seepage. Shame. Ralph hated life right now. He just wanted to die. He'd give anything to be back with Marshmallow, crying at her proposition, for here, no tears could flow.

He had to shimmy across the room to get some toilet paper. Jules' head hung low, showing that her shame was bad enough that she opted to be closer to the origin of the mess rather than suffer the indignity of looking Ralph in the eye. Ralph wiped and tossed the toilet paper in the trash.

He looked at the urinal, wondering what could be done. Nothing came to mind. Hopeless embarrassment was their only recourse.

The mint floated like a lily pad in a dark brown swamp. He tried flushing it, but that only added to the mess. Ralph sighed as his swamp became diluted. He flushed again, instantly regretting his actions as the mess overflowed the urinal. He took a few steps back to avoid the brown filth that began to drip onto the floor.

"Look, Jules," he said. "This, I mean, you know. This is messed up. I don't think I can even come up with the words to say how I feel right now."

Jules continued to stare at the floor as she wiped. "I know. Don't worry. I've got an idea."

Jules' confidence created confusion that helped Ralph forget his shame.

"Idea?" he asked. "What, do you have a time machine or something?"

Her signature grin returned to her face as she stood up from the toilet.

"Nope. Just as good. Let me text a guy." She didn't flush the toilet as she stood up.

Ralph opened the door to the bathroom. A man in a dress shirt, who appeared to be the manager, from the nametag on his shirt that read "Manager," was standing outside. He took a look in as the two, unfortunate souls exited the scene of the crime.

"What the hell did you do in there?" he asked.

"It was your food," replied Jules as they walked past him.

"Hey," the manager yelled, as they walked away. Ralph and Jules moved in a brisk walk.

"Hey," the manager called again. "Come clean this up. This is disgusting. Who do you think can ever use this bathroom again with this disgusting mess?"

"Not a chance," Ralph replied.

As they exited the Del Taco, the manager shouted, "Never come here again. I have to call the health department. You two are diseased."

"He's right you know. We are sick people," he said, as they reached Ralph's truck.

Jules pulled out a cigarette. "Most of the good ones are."

CHAPTER
Seven

THEY DROVE BACK TOWARD WEST COMPTON. JULES typed away on her phone as Ralph wondered what the hell she could be doing to help them get past the unfortunate bathroom incident. He assumed, since they were heading back to his neck of the woods, she'd be sleeping over. He wasn't sure how he felt about spending any more time with her.

"Okay good," Jules said, as she looked up from her phone. "He's got the stuff."

Ralph didn't like the sound of that.

"Stuff," he asked.

"Yea. So we can forget we got sick in the same fucking bathroom. Don't tell me that's something you want to remember for the rest of your life."

"No, but there's no such thing as a 'forget me not' pill."

"Silly clown, of course there is," Jules replied, as she put her hand on his leg.

They drove in silence for another twenty minutes, until

Jules told them to park on a side street. Ralph had done some pretty messed up shit under the influence of drugs in his life, but he liked to think that was one stage in his past he didn't constantly want to recreate.

"I don't like the looks of this," Ralph said. "Can't we just get really drunk instead?"

Jules giggled. "That's part two. Let's just wait for Cousin Bark to get here." Ralph stuttered again, completely taken aback by the name he'd just heard.

"Cousin Bark? Like tree bark?"

Jules gave him a puzzled glance. "No, like Cousin Bark."

A tall, Middle Eastern looking man, wearing a straw hat, approached the truck. He opened the driver's seat, causing Ralph to think they were being highjacked for a second before Jules waved at their new companion.

"Hello friends," Cousin Bark said. Ralph was squished in the middle, between them, wondering why Cousin Bark hadn't gone around to Jules' side, where he could instead violate the space of a familiar face.

"You got the goods?" Jules asked. Cousin Bark reached into his jacket pocket and pulled out a bag of pills.

"I sure do. Two Fruity Pebble salads. Uppers, downers, whatever you need to forget the trauma of the day. This day. Such tragedy."

Ralph wondered what Jules had actually told him about the incident.

"I'm Ralph by the way," he said, extending his hand.

Instead of shaking it, Cousin Bark embraced him in a hug. For the second time that day, Ralph wanted to die. Three more times and he'd break his old record.

"Bartholomew, but most call me Cousin Bark. It's a name my sister gave me back in Damascus." Ralph sat in silence, frustrated that he couldn't tell if his newfound "friend" was joking.

"These are on the house right? You still owe for the train job," Jules chimed in.

Ralph pretended not to hear her.

"You don't need to bring up past debts Jules," Cousin Bark answered. "I'm always there for those who need me. Now, I need to get going. I have tickets to the Kings game. You two get better, you hear me. Life is precious. Cherish it."

He gave Ralph another hug and leaned over him to give Jules a much more impersonal high five. He farted before leaving, making Ralph nauseous as he remembered the events of the past hour. Ralph rolled down the window as he slid back into the driver's seat.

"Nice guy right?" Jules asked, as he turned the ignition.

"Yes, wonderful. A modern day saint." He stopped himself from continuing as he realized how sarcastic he sounded. Cousin Bark did give them a bag of free drugs.

"Where to now?" he asked. "My place or yours?" Jules cackled.

"Please. Take us to that shithole bar you brought me to last week."

Ralph did a double take with his foot, as he was about to press on the gas.

"We are not taking a bunch of drugs and going to the Brimstone Saloon. My friends are there. Ouch!"

Jules pinched him. "Damn straight, we will. Step on it,

before I lose all attraction to you, clown. You're lucky a girl like me even talks to you."

Ralph knew she had a point, except for the fact that she was a complete nut. Something inside him warmed every time he looked at her. She reminded him of a Hot Pocket. Smoking hot on the outside with an icy interior.

Still, a repeat of Del Taco would deprive him of his prized hangout and possibly more importantly, his friends. Ralph tried to weight the pros and cons of Jules' plan before she grew angry and shouted, "Now Jango, before I push you out and steal your truck."

Ralph sighed as he put the truck into gear and drove off.

CHAPTER
Eight

"**O**H DEAR GOD," RALPH SAID, AS HE FELT THE PAIN IN his head intensify. "Where am I?" he called out. Something smelled awful. *Shit?* No, it was body odor. Body odor mixed with garbage left out to rot for ten years.

He looked around. His trailer. He'd made it back safely. There was a body in the bed next to him. It wasn't Jules. Shit.

He heard a groan next to him. Manuel.

"Oh fucker," his friend said. "What a night." Ralph rolled out of bed and hit the floor.

"What the fuck are you doing here?" Ralph replied.

"Fuck. My head. Motherfucker." Jules. She must have been sleeping on the other side of Manuel.

"Okay," Ralph said, as he tried to stand up. His knees were unresponsive and his mouth was drier than a BYU football tailgate. "Does anyone know what happened last night?"

He instantly regretted his words. The evidence pointed to a threesome. He liked Manuel, but only as a friend. Manuel was not an attractive man.

"The last thing I remember is the scared look on your face when Cousin Bark gave you that hug," said Jules. Ralph tried to remember whom she was talking about.

"The guy with the straw hat? Who could forget him?" Manuel sat up in the bed.

"What are you doing here?" Ralph asked. Manuel didn't answer.

"Well," Ralph pressed. "Answer me, you fucker." Manuel opened his mouth to speak, only to close it again. He did this two more times.

Finally, he said, "I'm not sure."

"Oh that's great," Ralph exclaimed, throwing him arms up. He stood up as he remembered something and looked out his window. He spotted his truck outside.

"Well, the truck is here. We're not in jail. That's something I guess." He scratched his rear, wondering if he'd be able to tell if Manuel had penetrated him. His rear did feel sore, but Ralph couldn't rule out his hemorrhoids as the cause of that discomfort. He remained unconvinced that he'd had sex with his friend.

"Well, that's good. What do we make of this then?" Manuel asked, after a delayed silence.

"Make of this?" Ralph answered. "What are you talking about?" Jules rolled over to look at both of them.

Manuel's eyes squinted at Ralph, possibly in anger at his friend.

"Sorry for addressing the elephant in the fucking room.

Didn't realize stating the obvious was going to be too hard for you to deal with."

Ralph turned red, fuming. "What the fuck are you even doing here in my home with my…," He paused.

"Go on, Jango," Jules said. "Your what?"

The red of Ralph's face turned to pink. "My princess," he sputtered out.

"Aww how cute," Jules said, who didn't appear to be phased at all by their peculiar situation.

Manuel slowly started to stand up.

"Okay, this got weird. Weirder. Fuck. You know what Ralph and Ralph's princess? I'm gonna go. I don't think anyone here knows what happened. That's probably for the best. I'm fine with never speaking of this again. You cool with that?"

Ralph nodded. "Yea. We're cool." Manuel reached over and shook Ralph's hand.

"My name's Princess Jules bitch," Jules yelled, as he started to walk out. Manuel didn't respond.

Ralph climbed back into bed, which smelled like cigarette, body odor, feces, cheese, cheap perfume, and rubbing alcohol.

"Jesus, what the hell happened yesterday?" he said, looking at Jules. He didn't really want to know.

"Fucking Cousin Bark man, he's got the good shit. I wonder why we even went to see him. I must have texted him or something."

An idea popped into Ralph's mind. He remembered why they'd sought out the services of Cousin Bark. *Del Taco.*

It all came back to him. The food. The shame. The manager. The evening no sane person would ever want to remember.

No person could call Jules sane, but she didn't remember either. He chose to keep it that way. Things were weird enough without bringing a double teamed round of diarrhea into the equation. He tried to remember why they'd gone there in the first place.

"Shit. Jules. The party. What time is it?" He spotted his phone on the floor. He picked it up and saw that it read 12:45.

"What time did you say the party was?" he asked. Jules rolled over in bed for a second.

"What party? Oh right. Three. Pretty sure. Yea."

Ralph stood up. His stomach growled, but he didn't think he could eat anything.

"We've got to get ready. Get up." He shook his princess. She kicked him.

"Stop that, give me five more minutes. Don't rush me asshole." Ralph wanted to protest, but then he caught a whiff of the smell in the air.

"Fine," he said. "I'm going to take a shower." He opened a window and headed to the bathroom.

The water was lukewarm. His hot water heater wasn't very good, but he felt more awake than he had before. He splashed some body wash on his skin, rinsing some unidentifiable crud off his stomach.

The bathroom door opened and Jules appeared. "Jesus Christ woman, does it ever end with you?" She climbed in the shower with him.

"Oh shut up, I don't want to have sex with you, you

freak of nature. This is a trailer. There isn't going to be any hot water left for me if I wait. There's barely any as it is. Get over yourself, clown."

He shared his body wash and squeezed what little shampoo he had left into Jules' hair. She took his hands and instructed him to massage the shampoo into her hair. He spent about a minute working her scalp when she abruptly said, "Okay that's good. Leave me to rinse. You've had your alone time in here already." She pushed him out of the shower.

Ralph didn't bother to protest. He brushed his teeth and headed into the kitchen. The shower had pumped some life back into him and with it, hunger. He opened his fridge to see what was inside.

Eggs, beer, butter, hot sauce, and a questionable looking tub of yogurt. He took the eggs and the butter out and found a frying pan. He used what was left in the carton, assuming Jules would either demand some or eat his if he didn't.

Ralph grew disgusted as he remembered his last meal, unless they'd eaten something on their drug bender. Shame, once again, filled his soul as he remembered what had happened bit by bit.

It didn't make any sense. Only, it sort of it did. Jules ordered enough food to feed a frat house. No wonder they both started shitting after exerting themselves immediately after. He wished he'd had some Pepto-Bismol on hand. He'd never make that mistake again.

He tried not to feel ashamed. He'd done worse things over the years. There's an old saying, "What happens in clown school stays in clown school," that sort of applied to this instance. Those days were supposed to be behind him though.

He started to question Jules' presence in his life. He didn't want to call her a destructive person but the label fit her better than just about anyone else he'd ever met. She behaved atrociously and showed little regard for anyone but herself.

How much did that matter? Ralph didn't think he could answer that as he fried his eggs. Part of his attraction to Jules came from loneliness. Deep down, he knew she had to feel the same way. She put up a strong front, but Ralph could see right through it. They both were two human beings cast aside by the rest of the world, called on only to serve as entertainment to brains that weren't even big enough to fully process what was right in front of them.

Imperfect as they were, there was strength in unity. He'd rather have bitchy Jules by his side than no one at all. At least, he hoped he would.

Jules came out wearing his bathrobe. He opted not to tell her how many times he'd masturbated wearing nothing but that without washing it once. All the times his sweaty asshole had rubbed up against the fabric. Jules didn't need to know that.

"Hungry?" he asked.

"Famished. I can't even remember the last thing I ate," she replied. He looked for hints of sarcasm in her tone and came up empty. If Jules remembered the Del Taco incident, she wasn't letting on.

He brought the eggs over and sat down.

"Is this it?" she asked, looking at her plate.

"Sorry," replied Ralph. "Didn't have time to go to the store to get the ingredients for a full Irish. My bad." She stared at her plate while Ralph went to put on a pot of coffee.

They ate in silence. Ralph's head started to hurt less as time wore on. Part of him dreaded performing. He'd put on countless shows, drunk, hung over, and on plenty of drugs. He once made an oak tree out of green and brown balloons while on LSD.

Ages ago. Forty-something Ralph didn't do those things. He just did his work and dealt with the depression that came from only being appreciated by people under the age of ten. Birthday parties are only happy for people who can't understand what aging really means.

"I'll put my face on here and then we can drive over to your place," he said to Jules as he ate his meager breakfast.

"Oh good," she replied. "I was getting tired of looking at you without it." He ignored her petty response.

Jules sat in the living/dining room while Ralph got dressed. She yelled a few times about how boring his apartment was. He had no defense. He needed to get a TV, or at least a functioning computer.

His phone vibrated. He had text from Sandra, his ex-wife.

"Ah shit," he called out loud, furious that he might have called her while he was all fucked up on Cousin Bark's Fruity Pebble salad. Looking at their chat history, he saw that he had not. "Thank God," he said to himself, pausing in fear at the thought that Jules had heard him. He knew

65

he needed to stop talking to himself with other people in his trailer.

Putting on his costume made him feel better about where he stood in life. Ralph had some shit to work out, but Jango the Clown was a fucking barrel of laughs. Being able to become someone else served as a nice escape for an otherwise pathetic existence.

He checked his bag, making sure his cards, balls, and other equipment were all present. Ralph used to get people to buy him drinks at the Brimstone by performing drunk tricks. It wouldn't have been surprising to see all his shit gone after the night they'd had, whatever night that might have been.

"All right, I'm good to go," he said. "Finally," replied Jules. "You take longer than a girl." He laughed.

"Of course I take longer, I'm a fucking clown."

"Damn straight Jango," Jules said, giving him a playful push.

He let out a quiet sigh that Jules, thankfully, didn't react to. He knew that Jules could be a hurtful careless sociopath. She could also be sweet. Ralph wondered if that was what kept him so attracted to her.

They got in Ralph's truck. "Aren't you forgetting something?" Jules questioned, causing Ralph to slam on the break.

"What?" he asked.

"Your clown nose silly," she said. "Put it on."

He always kept his clown nose in his pocket when he wasn't wearing it. It was a vintage model created by the late Jeremiah Longwiggles. Ralph liked it because it always stayed perfectly on his nose, while allowing him plenty of room to breathe. They didn't make noses like that anymore.

"I'm not putting it on."

"Oh yes you are," she replied. Ralph gave her a baffled look.

"What's your obsession with clowns anyway? I knew a couple circus groupies back in my day who had clown fetishes, but never someone your age."

Jules took a cigarette out of her purse and pretended to offer Ralph one.

"Don't you know how rude it is to talk about a woman's age? Besides, didn't you ever stop to think that the girls who used to have clown fetishes had to grow up sometime? Unless you're some sick fuck who thinks his audience lives in Peter Pan land. Wouldn't put it past old Jango."

Ralph started to put two and two together. Jules never called him by his actual name. Only Jango, or sometimes, clown.

"You saw my act, didn't you?" he said. "The old Fuzzy and Jango show." Smoke billowed out of Jules' mouth as she laughed and coughed.

"Oh please. Don't kid yourself. Even if I did see some children's circus act in the 80s, you think I'd remember it now? I don't even remember yesterday."

Ralph smiled like a true clown.

"We were on late night TV a few times. Wasn't just kids. You don't need to admit it. It's okay. Those were the days."

"What happened then? Where's good old Fuzzy? What kind of name is that anyway?" Jules' voice deepened, indicating genuine nuggets of interest hidden in her usual sarcasm.

"He died in the early 90s."

"I'm sorry to hear that," Jules said.

"You won't be sorry if you hear what did him in. You'll laugh louder than you ever have before," he said. Jules didn't answer.

"He got run over by a tractor one night while he was asleep in a pumpkin patch." Ralph waited for laughter that didn't come.

"You're kidding?"

"I shit you not. There was an all-night orgy up in Schenectady, New York at old MacGregor's place. Someone said the old fuck was always piss drunk and passed out by seven at night. So, Fuzzy and a couple of his buddies got some local girls and start fooling around with the vegetables and shit. Putting eggplant and zucchini up each other's asses. You know, real clown business. Anyway, the next morning, MacGregor is out there on his old tractor and that was the end of Fuzzy."

Jules offered him another cigarette, letting her hand linger on his for a moment as he accepted.

"That's absurd," she said. "I'm so sorry."

Ralph took a puff as he lit his cigarette and replied, "There's a lot of conspiracy theories about that night. Locals say MacGregor knew what went on in his crops and was looking to put an end to it. That explains why he brought his tractor into the pumpkin patch. Every person with half a brain knows not to bring a tractor anywhere near a pumpkin crop. The police never seriously looked into homicide because, well, they were all trespassing, but that bastard killed my friend."

"They," Jules replied. "Where were you?" Ralph took an especially long drag of his cigarette.

"We had a falling out. By the early 90s, people were starting to get a little tired of clowning. Superheroes were in and then later, that fucking clown wannabe Elmo. We needed to freshen up our act, but Fuzzy couldn't handle the passing of time. We split about a year or so before the accident. Never got to bury the hatchet."

Jules didn't answer. Ralph thought of happier days as they drove on to her place. *People always said to let the past go, but what happens when you're denied the opportunity?* Ralph missed Fuzzy, but that didn't change anything about where he currently found himself in life.

She gave him another cigarette as she walked inside. Ralph sat quietly and puffed. He looked at his phone, knowing he'd need to call his ex-wife sooner or later. She probably wanted money he didn't have and likely never would.

Manuel's earlier proposition came to mind. He thought about the Texas opportunity, the chance to get back into the swing of things. He knew his odds at actually getting a part were low. What he really wanted to know was how much that mattered to him, if the chance alone had value worth pursuing.

He looked at his phone again and saw that Jules had been inside for twenty minutes. He honked the horn. A faint, muffled expletive could be heard from the top floor of the house.

Five minutes later, the princess emerged. He could see why she took so long. She looked immaculate in her pink dress complete with layers of skirts and a face made up in a professional manner like someone who didn't have sex in Del Taco bathrooms.

"We're late," he said.

"Then fucking step on it," she replied. "No more cigarettes either, I'm not having this dress dry cleaned twice in six months." She grabbed what was left of his cancer stick, took a long drag, and tossed it out the window.

She looked at Ralph, who looked slightly different. "Nice nose, hot stuff," she said. Ralph's familiar erection returned as they drove off toward Beverly Hills.

CHAPTER
Nine

RALPH FIGURED THAT THE PARTY WOULD BE AT A NICE house. He didn't realize it'd be at a mansion that looked like something straight out of *Downton Abbey*. He started to think that Jules had been lowballed by accepting eighteen hundred.

He pulled up to the gate. A security guard gave his truck a disgusted look before staring at Ralph and Jules for what seemed like longer than necessary.

"I take it you're the entertainment," he said.

"Nah, the help," replied Ralph. He squeezed his nose in case the security guard took umbrage with his gag."

The security guard rolled his eyes.

"Make a left. The guesthouse garage door will be open. Please pull in. I mean no disrespect, but Mrs. Vasquez would not like the looks of your vehicle out in the open sir."

Ralph didn't know how that could be said without sounding disrespectful. He gave a defeated wave and pulled into the gate.

"I think your truck is a beauty, Jango," Jules said, as she tried to hold back giggles.

The house was one of the largest Ralph had ever seen in person. With the tall pillars and massive front steps, Ralph thought it might be five floors tall.

"Where the fuck are we?" he asked. "How'd you find these people Jules?"

He made a right and pulled into the open garage door, which opened on its own as they approached. He wondered if the security guard had opened it himself or if there was another employee paid solely to keep undesirable vehicles out of sight from the rest of the property. They stepped out of the car, unsure of where to go from there.

The door into the house opened and a girl wearing a headset entered the garage.

"Jango the Clown and Princess Aurora?" she asked. Ralph nodded. "My name's Dandelion, I'm Mr. Vazquez's executive assistant."

"A pleasure," Jango said, as he gave her hand a kiss. Jules shot him a dirty look.

"Mr. Vasquez grew up in Houston sir. He used to see your act all the time. I can't express how thrilled he is to have you here." Ralph returned Jules' disdainful facial expression with a smug one of his own.

"Wonderful," replied Ralph.

"So, the party starts in about forty-five minutes. We've set catering up on the first floor, but the second is all yours. The tables and helium tanks are all set up in the backyard. I'll come in to give you the five-minute warning for your introduction. Can I get you anything? Sparkling water, coffee, smoothie?"

"We'll take two of the bubbly waters," Jules said. Ralph thought about asking for a beer, but decided against it. It didn't matter that the host was an old fan. Openly drinking at a children's party was always frowned upon.

He felt his headache start to vanish as he took a whiff of the garage. A place that should carry the scents of oil and spilled paint smelled fresh and alive. Ralph thought it must be the smell of money.

The catering also smelled like money. He spotted bowls of meatballs and lobster tails as they walked up the stairs. Jules sat down on one of the beds as they reached a room almost too big to call a bedroom, which was larger than Ralph's whole trailer.

"Oh my God, feel this mattress. This is what these people bought for their fucking guests. Can you believe it?"

Ralph put his hand on the mattress, which reminded him of what a kitchen dishtowel felt like while he was tripping on acid back in the 70s. Only this mattress didn't require psychedelic drugs to feel like the softest fucking thing he'd ever touched.

"I can't believe no one regularly lives here," he said. "Now I know where I'm going to go if there's ever a zombie attack." Jules began to inspect the pillows that looked to also be of very high quality.

Dandelion returned with their beverages.

"Do you think I could get a plate of that food? I hate to clown on an empty stomach." Ralph said, accepting his bubbly water with glee.

Dandelion put her hand over the mic on her headset

before replying.

"Normally, I'd have to say no, but since this is a children's party and Mr. Vasquez is such a big fan, I don't think he'd mind feeding a childhood idol." Ralph thought of something as Dandelion headed back down the stairs.

"How is it that you booked this gig if I'm the one she keeps talking about?" Ralph asked as Jules laid down on the especially soft mattress. He turned to face her. "Well," he persisted.

Jules didn't answer.

"Oh come on princess. Out with it." She looked at him like a child trying to deny having eaten all the cookies even though the chocolatey evidence was all over her face.

"If you didn't wreck your computer jacking off, you'd know how to do a basic Google search. I looked you up jackass. Knew you'd performed all over, but that Houston was your home base for a long time. Vasquez wanted an act with a clown and, well, I googled him too. Turns out he's also from Texas. Did I have a clue he'd know who you were? Of course not, but I called him up and said I had a joint act going with Jango the Clown of 'Fuzzy & Jango' and here we are. I'm not stalking you or anything, it's just good business. It'd do you some good to learn a thing or two about that."

Ralph didn't know what to feel as his mind became flooded with emotions. Vulnerable, for having his private information exposed on the internet. Impressed, that Jules thought to do some research on him. Frustration, that she'd kept secrets from him. Anger, that Mr. Vasquez lowballed them after finding out that Jango was part of the act.

"Fair enough," he said. "Except for one thing. You left

me out. What the fuck Jules?"

She sat up in the bed. "Yeah. I did. I'm not going to make excuses." Ralph's jaw dropped. He adjusted his nose, afraid that holding in his rage would cause it to blow up.

"Excuse me," he said. Jules opened her purse and shut it again. He thought she might be reaching for a cigarette as some kind of nervous tic.

"I'm not going to apologize. I tried to pull a fast one and you caught me. You forget, we've only known each other for a week. You and me, we're not a team. Not yet at least. I'm a broke, shitty, children's birthday party performer. I tried to make a few extra bucks in a slightly, unethical fashion. Sue me."

Ralph could see things from Jules' perspective. Clowns ripped each other off all the time. He'd poached plenty of gigs over the course of his career.

"I get it, but you're a terrible negotiator," he said. "If you'd let me handle it, we'd both have more money. Learn from this you fucking idiot." He thought he heard footsteps and hoped Dandelion hadn't heard his profanity. The sound turned out to be an exotic parakeet pecking at a diamond encrusted birdfeeder outside the window.

He ate his food while Jules rummaged around in the bathroom.

"Find anything?" he asked, as he bit into some soft shell crab. He wondered why he'd waited this long to try something this good. He prayed he didn't have soft shell crabs after sharing a bed with Manuel.

"Yea," Jules answered. "Couple bottles of Xanax, some Ambien. Bunch of different names on the labels. Holy shit.

I recognize one of them. A host on some cable TV show. Oh God, clown, you'll never believe what I found."

Ralph cared more about his food than whatever Jules' had discovered in a guest bathroom. "I don't care," he said.

She emerged from the bathroom holding a very large strap-on dildo.

"What the hell is that doing in there?" he asked. Ralph knew what she had on her mind; dirty thoughts.

"No, put that away," he said. She walked over to his bag. "Not in there. Jesus. What the hell is wrong with you?"

She held it up, continuing not to speak. "No Jules. Get that thing away from me." She left it on the bed as she put the pill bottles in her purse.

"Aren't you going to say anything?" he asked.

"Why, when watching you squirm is so much fun?"

Ralph saw her point. "Yeah, I don't want you to get any ideas."

"Says the clown who woke up with a man in his bed. Oh please, won't it be fun?"

He couldn't believe what he was hearing. "Fun. For who? No. My backdoor is strictly exit only."

Jules stuck out her tongue.

"Gross," Ralph said, as he tried to block out what must be on her mind. She bunched up the strap-on and added it to her collection of contraband in her purse.

Ralph finished his plate and felt his stomach rumble a bit.

"Be right back," he said, as he looked for a bathroom further away from them to take a dump. He didn't want to trigger Jules' memory at all.

He sat on the toilet and thought about Jules' character. She lied to him and wanted to put a huge dildo up his ass. He tried to come up with a single good reason to keep her in his life. None came to mind.

And yet, the idea that he should tell her to take a hike hadn't really presented itself either. She might be a horrible person, but she was his horrible person. He almost fell off the toilet as he considered the situation.

As Ralph exited the bathroom, he thought of something rather important. They hadn't prepared their show at all. He presumed that she knew how to put on a good time for the kids without vulgarities, but they were a joint act now. They needed to be able to act like one.

"Have you thought about the show?" he asked. She looked up from a magazine she'd found on the side table.

"No. I figured you were the pro and I'd just follow your lead. Is that fucking all right with you, boss?" she replied.

"Sort of. What tricks can you do?" Her eyes squinted together and she threw her arms up in the air. "Tricks? I'm not a clown, I'm a princess. I don't do tricks. I paint people's faces and I twirl my wand around and act all cute. Maybe a couple songs and a game of Simon Says."

Ralph thought for a second.

"Okay. Have you worked as an assistant before?" "Assistant? Newsflash Jango. Princesses aren't servants. I shouldn't have to tell you that."

Ralph sighed. "No, not like that. I just need you to help me out with a couple things. You can do your face painting, but we'll need more than that to satisfy a guy like Vasquez if he really wants to see Jango the Clown in action."

She bit her lip. "If you say so. I don't see why you'd pull out all the stops for a guy who ripped us off, but your call. I wouldn't want you to feel emasculated not being able to put on a proper show for those snot nosed brats."

Ralph laughed as he thought about Mr. Vasquez and his negotiating strategies.

"Leave him to me," he said.

Dandelion returned shortly after they'd finished their "meeting."

"Mr. Vasquez wants you both outside to get ready," she said.

"It's show time princess," Ralph said, as he returned to the bathroom to check his appearance. His wig was on straight and he had his finest purple polka dotted suspenders on. Ralph took a deep breath, adjusted his nose again, and walked outside.

The Vasquez' backyard made the house where he'd first met Jules look like an abandoned lot frequented by drug dealers and prostitutes. The kind of place you'd expect to see Cousin Bark and Marshmallow hanging around. They had a swimming pool that looked like a rainforest oasis. A stone waterfall was decorated with exotic plants and a hot tub that could have been excavated from a hot spring in the Grand Canyon. The lawn was immaculately maintained, perhaps even to the point of being illegal. Ralph wondered how Vasquez rigged his sprinklers to supply enough water for such a paradise.

Ralph looked at their table. There were two helium tanks next to it. He looked at Jules and said, "Why don't you handle filling the balloons and I'll tie them?" Jules watched

Dandelion until she walked out of earshot.

"Sure. Why don't you just do the show alone if you're going to turn into some bossy asshole," she responded.

Ralph did his best clown smile imaginable, showing off his whitish brown teeth and his makeup-accented eyebrows.

"Admit it. You like it when I take charge."

She waved her wand at him and said, "You'll pay for that one clown. Believe me."

Ralph shuddered as he thought of what she could possibly have in mind.

CHAPTER
Ten

THE PARTY STARTED WITHOUT ANY PROBLEMS. RALPH did his juggling and even managed to keep a straight face while Jules sang a horrible rendition of a song from some stupid kid's movie. His clown makeup worked wonders toward concealing his amusement.

He performed a few card tricks and some basic magic. The kids cheered and cheered, though their faces really seemed to light up when Jules spoke. Jules might be a fairly trashy woman, but Princess Aurora reeked of class. Not in the same way her counterpart reeked of Tex-Mex while in the middle of diarrhea.

The children laughed. The one face that Ralph consistently watched belonged to Mr. Vasquez. The man sat in the back wearing a seersucker suit and never took his eyes off Ralph, even when Jules commanded the attention of the rest of the audience.

Ralph knew exactly what the man wanted. Vintage Jango. He'd probably watched old YouTube clips, whatever ones existed. This wasn't the time or the place for that kind of talent.

After balloon animals, Ralph announced that Jules was to begin the face painting. He turned to take a sip of water while the partygoers swarmed around his companion. As he took a refreshing glug, he heard a voice call out, "What do you have planned for the finale?"

Mr. Vasquez.

"Finale," replied Ralph, who tried not to laugh at the unusually formal term for a birthday party performance. "Usually, it's just time for cake. Hard to compete with all that sugar, you know?"

By the blank look on Mr. Vasquez' face, Ralph started to suspect that he didn't know. "Really? That's it? You used to breathe fire. I watched a clip of you doing battle with a lion armed with nothing but a foam finger. Fucking hysterical. How can there be no big finale after all you've done?" Vasquez eyed Ralph like an unsatisfied Applebee's customer, upset that their burger was well done instead of rare, an option not offered by most casual dining restaurants.

"The kids don't respond well to the old acts. Especially not fire, with all they've been told about stop, drop, and roll and all that shit, you know?" Ralph took another sip of his water to keep from socking his ungrateful employer.

"Actually, despite your persistent attempts to get me to agree with you, I don't know," Mr. Vasquez said. "You see, I paid you two a lot of money to put on a show. And it's been cute and all that, but I've been sitting back there thinking to myself, what did I really pay two grand for? Some juggling and face paint? You can see where I'm coming from?"

Ralph tried not to laugh as he saw his job becoming more and more difficult. Before he could answer, Mr. Vasquz added, "I even got you a unicycle in case you didn't have one. You know, the one act where you used to juggle those flaming torches before you passed them off to your partner. What was his name, Frankie?"

"Fuzzy and it wasn't two grand." Ralph sensed a standoff brewing between these two not so dissimilar figures. A clown in full makeup and one hiding in a different kind of suit. Ralph had a mind to walk off right then and there. It wouldn't be the first time he'd left a party before the final act, though it would be the first time he'd walked out sober.

Only, something stopped him. "I'll make you a deal. You pay me something respectable, not that eighteen-hundred-dollar bullshit you conned my assistant into and you go get that unicycle. I'll show this party something you won't forget."

Vasquez looked him up and down, saving an especially, large grin for his big clown shoes.

"You've got yourself a deal Jango." He motioned for Dandelion to come over.

Ralph walked over to Jules.

"What was that all about?" asked Jules as she painted a frog on a girl's cheek.

"The grand finale," he replied. "Listen, can you juggle at all?"

She smudged the frog a bit. "Juggle? Who said anything about juggling?" she asked, as she dipped her paintbrush in water to rectify the mess. Ralph turned away.

"Shit," was the only word on his mind as he tried to

come up with a plan. He leaned over to Jules again and said, "Don't worry. Just follow my lead."

He walked to the other side of the table to retrieve his bag. He picked up five of his bounciest balls and gave them a cold, hard look. The balls looked to be staring him down as well while he formulated his grand finale.

When the last kid received a poorly crafted animal on her face, Jules stood up. He spotted Dandelion with the unicycle.

"Okay, everyone, who's ready for the big finale? Boy, has Jango got a surprise for you." He stopped to try to remember the birthday kid's name. He drew a blank, but he didn't let it get to him.

"It appears children, that one among you has been a fan of Jango's for a very, long time. Do you know who that might be?"

"Jesus," called out a boy.

"Almost," Ralph replied, squeezing his nose to receive some extra laughter. "Can Mr. Vasquez come to the front to assist with the grand finale?"

Mr. Vasquez and Dandelion made their way to Ralph's work station. Ralph looked at the crowd again. "We already saw some juggling, but that was only a warm up. Who wants to see some real hardcore juggling?" The crowd went wild.

He motioned for the unicycle. "Now, this will be a three-part performance. My lovely assistant Princess Aurora is wearing a gown made out of magic fabric, which repels anything that touches it. Like these balls here." He stopped to regain composure after mentioning Jules and balls in the same sentence.

Ralph modified this trick from an old one he and Fuzzy used to perform. Duel unicycle juggling was a sight to see, especially on evenings when they used flaming torches. Unfortunately, Jules didn't know how to juggle so she'd need to be used as a human prop instead.

"Mr. Vasquez will help pass me my magic balls while I juggle them with the help of the back of Princess Aurora's magic dress. I'll start with one."

He looked at the unicycle, trying to remember the last time he'd been on one, let alone ridden it wearing clown shoes. "Just like riding a bicycle," he told himself. He motioned for Jules to turn her back to him. She gave him a look of pure disgust.

He climbed on the unicycle and took a second to check his balance. He knew this would either work really well, or he'd be laughed at by a bunch of children. Normally clowns were supposed to like that, but this carried a certain make or break sentiment to it that Ralph wanted to fully comprehend before attempting this stunt.

This wasn't just about the party or the extra cash. Ralph saw a crisis of identity stand before him. Ralph could perform at children's birthday parties. That part was easy. He needed Jango to really impress the masses.

He put his right foot on the pedal and kicked up. The grass gave him plenty of cause for worry, but he'd ridden much shittier unicycles under much shittier conditions. The lawn should be the one worried about getting all fucked up from his peddling prowess.

Riding took some getting used to. He sputtered a bit forward and countered by taking a lap around the table. He squeaked his nose a few times to get some cheap laughs and to take the crowd's mind off his struggles.

He juggled his sole ball a few times. Feeling the awkward motion of the singular piece of rubber, he said, "I think it's time to add another. Mr. Vasquez, please."

He threw a ball to Ralph. It was a bit lower than he would have liked, but Ralph caught it and didn't miss a beat. The crowd clapped as his balls swung in a clockwise motion in the air.

He pivoted the unicycle to face the crowd, with his back facing Mr. Vasquez. "Two is nice and all, but three's a crowd. We like crowds, don't we? Mr. Vasquez, on the count of three, one more over my right shoulder please. One, two, three." The ball arrived perfectly into the rotation. The crowd roared with applause.

The unicycle didn't completely cooperate as he attempted to turn toward Jules. He had to peddle backwards a bit to regain control. Peddling a little too fast, he backtracked to make sure no balls were left behind.

Jules' pink back served as an adequate target. "Watch children as Jules' dress repels my magic balls of fury." As soon as his left hand tossed one ball up in the air, his right hand tossed another at Jules' back. He kept the two in rotation going as the ball hit the middle of her back and returned toward him.

Now for the tricky part, he thought, for a split second. The ball curved more toward his torso than he would have liked. He peddled forward slightly and reached to the middle of his chest to intercept the ball. He tossed it upwards as soon as he caught it and let himself breathe as the he got back into his juggling rhythm.

A few kids gave him a standing ovation.

"How'd you like that?" he asked to a chorus of cheers. "That was a little easy. How about four balls? Mr. Vasquez." The man stood off to the side of him. He had a smile on his face like a kid in a candy store, about to get a mouthful of cavities. He slow tossed a fourth ball into the mix, almost causing Ralph to topple over on his unicycle as he struggled to maintain his balance.

"Hit her again," yelled a boy. Ralph could only imagine what Jules was thinking at this moment. "Now, now, children it's not hitting. Princess Aurora's dress protects her. It's a reflection. Isn't that right Princess?"

Jules gave a thumbs up.

"What do princesses do when they're confronted with evil?" she replied.

"They use their wands," said a girl.

"That's right," replied Jules. "If the dress doesn't protect them, the wand certainly will." Her eyes pierced Ralph as if that was directed at him.

Ralph bounced some balls off Jules back a few more times, adding the fifth ball into the mix. When the act had run its course, he said, "And now Princess Aurora is going to catch the balls with her hat. Let's cheer her on."

Jules turned to face him and scowled as she removed her large pointy hat. Ralph lobbed the balls in the air one by one. Jules caught the first four, but let the last one drop. "Can't let it get away," she said as she scurried over to grab it out of the grass.

"Let's give three cheers for Princess Aurora, Jango

the Clown, and Mr. Vasquez," Dandelion said, as Ralph dismounted from his unicycle. The children cheered and cheered. Ralph didn't want to think about how sweaty he'd become.

"Time for cake kids," a woman said, presumably Mrs. Vasquez. The children all headed toward a few, long tables decorated with *Thomas the Tank Engine* and *Power Ranger* tablecloths. Ralph handed Dandelion the unicycle.

"Well, well, well that was mighty impressive Jango," Mr. Vasquez said. He pulled out his checkbook. Jules walked over with an angry look on her face.

"You've certainly earned a little extra," he added.

"A little extra," Ralph said. "You know how difficult that trick was? Did it all for you hotshot. A private performance like that from a household name is pure gold. Try doubling our rate for the day."

Jules grinned at Ralph. "Plus a hundred for the dry cleaning of my dress after I had to be pelted with that dirty rubber." Vasquez gave them a mischievous look, like he'd just gotten the cashier at the frozen yogurt shop to give him an extra stamp on his rewards card.

"Twenty-five hundred, plus fifty for the dress," he said. "Only because you brought back fond childhood memories of me with my father and his mistress. You two are cute together. The princess and the clown. Who would have thought?" He handed Ralph the check and patted him on the back.

CHAPTER
Eleven

"**T**HAT WAS HUMILIATING, YOU KNOW," JULES SAID, AS they drove out the gate. "What's that supposed to teach women, having balls bounced off my back by a creep riding a unicycle?"

Ralph laughed as he smoked a cigarette. "Jules. We perform at children's birthday parties. Move beyond shame. This whole business is embarrassing. Get over it. We got paid."

"Yea, we got paid, less than what you were asking. Some negotiator you are."

Ralph shook his head.

"You want to try and criticize me after what I did back there? Do you know how hard that trick was to pull off? You had the easy part. I don't know why you're whining about the money either after you stole a couple hundred bucks worth of pills."

She took a pill out of her purse, put it in her mouth, and took another drag of her cigarette before she swallowed.

"Gross," said Ralph as he watched her. "Why do you even do that anyway? Can't we celebrate like normal people?"

She giggled. "Sure we can, but you didn't let me have any fun in the guest house. Tell you what. We go back to your place to have some fun and afterwards, you can buy me dinner like some so-called normal person. Deal?"

Ralph knew not to trust Jules' idea of deals but he agreed. They'd made quite a bit of money and he wanted to spend some of it on a decent steak. His success had him hornier than ever, which made it okay that they were having dessert before the main course.

He laughed to himself as he thought about how alive he felt on that stupid unicycle, tearing apart some rich asshole's lawn. Nothing about it besides the stupid one wheeled transport should've reminded him of the olden days, but it had. He thought back to when his craft made him happy and didn't just serve as his pathetic means for survival.

"How'd I'd look while I was riding?" he asked.

"How should I know, I had my back to you asshole," she replied.

"I looked good, I know it," he said.

"Keep talking like that and I'm going to have to add that to your punishment list."

He didn't ask about the list as they drove on toward his trailer. It didn't sound fun, or real, for that matter. He knew not to question the limits of Jules' insanity.

They reached the trailer. Ralph sat down in his chair as soon as they walked inside. Jules went to rummage in his fridge, clinking some glass together and doing something that Ralph probably didn't want to know about.

His reservations didn't stop him from asking, "What are you looking for? I know I need to go to the grocery store."

She shut the fridge door, walked over to him, and ran her finger up his trousers.

"No, that's okay. You've got everything I need. Now, go in the bedroom."

Something inside him told him to say no. He didn't. He knew how hard she could make him with simple words. He stood up and walked to the bedroom. As he opened the door, he looked back at Jules.

"You coming," he said. She had an evil grin on her face.

"In a minute clown."

The bedroom smelled less like death than it had when he first woke up. He knew he needed to go to the laundromat to wash his sheets. He hadn't cleaned them in weeks. He tried his best to purge that tiny detail from of his mind.

He laid down on the bed with his face buried in the pillow. As much as he wanted sex, he couldn't help but let out a yawn of exhaustion. It had been a stressful twenty-four hours.

His mattress smelled like someone tried to cook an assortment of rotted fruit and cottage cheese inside it. He didn't know who to blame. Manuel stood out as the easy target, but he remembered how much grime had rinsed off in the shower. He wondered what they'd gotten up to on all those drugs, or if he'd even want to know.

He thought about rolling over to see what the hold up was, but he remained on his stomach. He heard footsteps and his arousal returned.

"Oh good, you've already assumed the position," she said.

"Position? What?" Ralph rolled over and looked at Jules, who stood before him wearing only her lingerie and the strap-on she'd found back at the guesthouse. She resembled a femme fatale from one of those trashy 70s movies they used to show in back alley theatres.

"Jules, no," he said. "I told you already. Put that dirty thing away." He crawled up to the top of his bed, as far away from her as he could possibly get.

"I know, but that was before you embarrassed me at the party. You liked that, didn't you?" She spoke with seduction, puckering her lips and licking them with her tongue.

"Jules, it was all for the act. You know that. We got seven hundred more out of it plus the dry cleaning. Come on."

She grabbed her rubber penis, harnessed across her shape wear. "I know. For the act. Except one of us got to thrust balls at the other and I don't think that's very fair. Do you, clown? This little toy has balls too. You bossed me around all afternoon. Is that how you think this works? Are you the only one who gets to thrust balls?"

Ralph let out a whimper as Jules stroked her rubber testicles.

"No," he replied.

"Good," said Jules. "I know you like things up there. Most men do, they just don't like to admit it. There's a G-spot or something. Feels good."

Ralph stopped to think about what she meant.

"What do you mean, you know I like it? What do you

91

remember about last night?"

She cackled and spanked her rubbery genitalia.

"I can call Manuel if you'd like. Someone needs to put you in your place. Who's it going to be clown?"

He started to take his clown nose off.

"No," she said. "Leave it on. You've been a very, naughty clown today. You've been bossy and you threw shit at me. It's time you learned who runs things around here. Do you understand that?"

Ralph nodded. "Yes," he said.

"Good. Now I want you to turn around." He turned around and assumed a tabletop position. His knees trembled against the soiled mattress.

"Excellent," she said. "I knew you liked that."

Ralph chose not to respond directly. Instead, he asked, "You've got lube right?"

She spanked his ass "Oh I've got lube all right. You're in good hands Jango. Princess always takes care of her clown."

Ralph put his head in between his hands. He wanted to hate what was happening. For good reasons, except for one. His erection had grown larger. He squeezed his knees together in an attempt to conceal it, not considering that this would only draw more attention to the region.

She peaked around his body. "Oh, enjoying this are we? I knew it. It's okay," she said.

He heard her open a bottle and felt relieved that she kept her promise to lube up. Perhaps this would be enjoyable after all.

"You ready clown?" she asked.

As he nodded, he felt himself become filled. She'd been

right about one thing. He did enjoy it, to the extent that his heterosexual masculinity could tolerate. He imagined Manuel and Jeffrey hearing about this, before shuddering. Manuel might have firsthand experience with the subject.

The feelings of pleasure started to intensify. Literally. Ralph felt a burning sensation in his lower, backside region.

"Is this supposed to burn Jules?" he asked.

"Not usually," she replied.

He turned his head as if to say, "What does that mean?" and then his eyes showed him the answer. He spotted his bottle of hot sauce on the floor.

"Jules, what the fuck? No. Tell me you didn't." He tried to crawl away but she laid on top on him, thrusting forward like an old lady at her aerobics class.

"You wanted lube clown. I gave you lube. This is your punishment for thinking you could boss your princess around. You didn't think I'd let you get away with that, did you?"

He couldn't respond. The fire inside him burned worse than if his entire crotch region served as a convention center for dancing lice. The pain filled every fiber of his clownish existence. Tears streamed down his face, like the ending of *Toy Story 3*.

But not tears of pain, not necessarily. Ralph never considered himself to be a masochist but this new turn of events forced him to question his existence. He thought Jules might be exactly what he needed after a day spent reliving his glory years.

"You're enjoying yourself, I know it," she said.

"Yes, princess," Ralph replied.

93

"Good clown, good." She spoke in a sinister voice, like a DMV employee denying a customer on the grounds of a minuscule typo after a four-hour wait.

Ralph likened these sensations to the satisfaction of successfully popping all the pimples on the left side of his face. The fluid that oozed out of them couldn't be all that different from the hot-sauced, induced seepage spilling out his back door. If this was wrong, then wrong was the new right.

Jules increased her tempo, moving back and forth in a fashion similar to someone trying to get a shopping cart up a steep ramp. In this case, the resistance brought forward by Ralph's rump served as a mere obstacle for her to move past in motions that caused her to use muscles in her hip region like she was trying out a barre fitness Groupon for the first time.

Ralph knew that what was happening was something that no person could ever fully comprehend. The image of a clown with tears down his face being penetrated by a forty-something, lingerie-clad deity might be enough to make a person of a careful disposition vomit. Their ballet of sorts didn't need to be appreciated by the outside world.

Two beings functioned in relative unity, that is, until Ralph emptied his cargo and fell forward onto his bed. His own fluid served as pomade for his chest hair. Jules slid out of him and unbuckled her strap-on.

"It ain't over yet clown," she said. "Eat me out and then let's get some dinner. This can be your appetizer."

Ralph's insides still quaked with the fire of the hot sauce. He had flashbacks to the time he'd contracted gonorrhea in clown school. He took solace in the fact that the burning would go away naturally and that the seepage would be relatively fit for human consumption if the situation called for it. Jules might be into that kind of stuff.

She rolled him over. Ralph tried to get a grip on what had happened as she climbed on top of him. He gave up as her damp, moist, bat cave blocked out the light.

CHAPTER
Twelve

Ralph walked into the Brimstone Saloon for the first time in four days, a new record for the year. He didn't have a proper excuse for his absence to tell Jeffrey either. The fear of embarrassment over anyone finding out what had happened with Jules loomed over him for days.

He also feared that he might have been unwelcome there after the incident with Jules, Manuel, and the pills from Cousin Bark. Memories from that part of the evening had not returned. Part of him hoped they wouldn't. That day carried such weird connotations.

Ralph had experienced some of his personal, greatest triumphs and biggest embarrassments for the year, all in a twenty-four hour span. He'd woken up next to one of his best friends, on a mattress that needed to be thrown away, but he'd also put on his greatest performance in at least five years. He'd had sex with Jules, but after she had fucked him in the ass with a strap-on. His achievements were clouded in some pretty weird shit. He wondered if that was the way it was supposed to be.

He hadn't seen much of Jules over the past few days. Twice to be exact. He called her once to get some food, which he of course paid for. Jules called him the other time to be eaten out, which she wanted to happen in the back of his truck, in a Target parking lot, at two in the morning.

Ralph found the act mildly thrilling, but he almost had a heart attack when a homeless man asked for a dollar while he was in the middle of performing cunnilingus. Jules screamed, which should have terrified Ralph but, he instead felt thankful that she didn't ask the man to join them.

Since then, he'd avoided her a bit. She'd asked him to accompany her to court on a day when he had a gig at a veterinary hospital and to "hang out," another evening when he and Manuel went to watch a Ratt tribute band perform at a club in Santa Monica. He wished he missed her more than he actually did.

Being with her made him feel alive but being apart was also liberating. He knew that many normal relationships caused people to feel this way. Then again, Jules and he didn't have a normal relationship. Ralph thought he wanted to keep it this way but part of him didn't really know what he wanted.

He spotted Manuel sitting at the bar, which bode well for him not being banned. He still didn't know when Manuel joined the fray. Chances were that Ralph didn't do anything stupid without his friend at his side. Making eye contact with Jeffrey made him stop in his tracks.

"Well, well, well. The prodigal clown returns," the aged

bartender said.

"Does that entitle me to a free drink?" Ralph asked, taking a seat next to Manuel.

"Sure, but the next one will cost you double. You owe me five bucks for the cab ride back to the bar. Manuel here already paid his share. I was worried he'd told you about it and you'd skipped town, you fucking cheapskate," Jeffrey said, shaking his head.

Ralph's heart sank. He had been an idiot after all. He opened his wallet and put a ten on the table.

"Thanks for that," he said. "Can I ask you what happened that night?"

Jeffrey let out a huge laugh. "Ha. Doesn't surprise me a bit that you don't remember." He paused, causing Ralph to wave his hand to motion for his friend to continue.

"You were maybe the easiest to deal with of the three of you. You, your broad, and the hot shot sitting next to you tried to get some fucking rave or something started here. Music wasn't even that loud. You were falling all over the place. I didn't know what to do, so I put you in one of the booths and you just kind of sat there while Jules and Manuel grinded up against each other and, occasionally, no one at all."

Ralph glared at Manuel.

"Thanks a lot for that, buddy."

"You were the one who insisted I take the pills with you. Said you couldn't do them all yourself. My hands are clean of all of this," Manuel replied, clinking his glass against Ralph's.

Ralph turned his gaze to Jeffrey.

"Did we do anything stupid?" Jeffrey paused and poured a drink of his own.

"You specifically? Besides practically drugging yourself into oblivion, nothing really that I imagine you wouldn't have done sober. You said some shit about Sandra and your kid, but I see drunks who do that all the fucking time. Manuel here, he puked in the urinal." Ralph laughed for reasons that neither of his friends could understand.

"Yea, laugh it up Ralph, your hands are really clean in this one buddy," Manuel said.

Ralph thought of a name that, rather surprisingly, had barely been mentioned.

"What about Jules?" he asked. Jeffrey turned away ominously. "What'd she do?" Ralph added, not sure that he wanted to hear the answer.

"Oh, she hit on some guys. Nothing too out of the ordinary. I didn't say anything because I couldn't really be sure the two of you were an exclusive thing and after hearing how Manuel got involved, I'm still highly skeptical. She danced by herself and with Manuel for a bit.

The real trouble began when the three of you went outside."

Ralph sighed.

"Oh dear."

Manuel clanked his glass down. "Oh dear is right. We could have been arrested. That woman is crazy."

Ralph looked up at Jeffrey, who nodded in agreement with Manuel.

"I found the two of you dumpster diving for old tacos. Had to bribe you to get out with burgers I never ended up buying. I called you guys a cab, but I realized I had to take you back myself when she threw a brick through a car window."

Ralph almost fell off his stool.

"Dear God," he said. Manuel tried not to laugh. "That's not all of it buddy."

Ralph almost got up and left, but he knew he had to hear what she'd done.

Jeffrey left to get a table another round.

"Tell me Manuel, I know you know." Manuel refused to comply. "I'm not telling you without Jeffrey here. I owe him that, after he cleaned up my puke. Shit's embarrassing Ralph."

Ralph sucked down the rest of his beer before Jeffrey could return. The altruistic bartender refilled his drink and said, "She shit on the car with the shattered windshield. Pulled her panties down and took a dump on it right then and there. Never seen anything like it. Didn't even see any blood on her feet after squatting in that glass either. I told her to stop and she walked over and shoved her underwear right down my shirt. Told me to enjoy sniffing them at night while she slept with the two of you. That was when I got your keys and drove you guys out of there. You're both lucky. There's no way I would have paid the bail for your sorry asses."

Ralph wanted to be surprised. To have this news hit him like Jules did whenever he said something she didn't like. To be knocked over like the windshield after Jules has tossed a brick through it, but the emotion escaped him.

Silence ensued. Ralph didn't know what to say. He

didn't know what should be said.

"I'm sorry."

Jeffrey patted him on the shoulder. "Don't be sorry. Not to me at least. I wouldn't be sorry to whoever owned that car either. They'd just kick shit out of you, rightfully so. We all meet crazy people Ralph, especially in your line of work. Don't give her a second thought."

Jeffrey departed once again to tend to some customers. Ralph sat defeated at the bar.

"Don't worry about Jules, Ralph. She was fun while she lasted."

Ralph glared at his friend.

"Fun while she lasted? Who's saying we broke up? We had sex that same day after you left. Shows how much you matter in the grand scheme of things, buddy."

Before Manuel could respond, Ralph felt his phone vibrate. He glanced at it and saw his ex-wife's name across the screen.

"Could this day get any fucking worse?" he said, as he exited the bar to take the call.

The heat of an unusually warm, May evening created almost as much sweat on Ralph's brow as the stress that his two friends had imposed upon him. He answered the phone with one hand while he rummaged around for a cigarette in his pocket with the other.

"Hello Sandra." He pulled the phone away from his ear as he lit the cigarette. Sandra never approved of his smoking as she considered it a terrible waste of money.

Ralph thought the same thing about makeup that wasn't used for clowning.

"Hey. I thought I'd check in and see how you were doing. It's been about a month."

Ralph knew what emotion she wanted him to feel. Guilt.

"I know. I need to call more. Natalie is never there when I call."

"Don't pin this on her. She has a life. Hasn't seen you in years, not that it matters to you."

"I know. I'm sorry. Is there a specific reason you called or was it just to make me feel like a piece of shit?"

"Don't pretend like you actually care Ralph. You'll be perfectly fine in about ten minutes. Always are."

He wanted to hang up the phone but he remembered his bank account statement.

"Look, I know you want money. I've got some cash to send over. I know I'm behind on alimony, but I did some shows," he said.

He heard a sigh.

"It's okay Ralph. Keep the money. I met a guy. I think I told you about him last month. Byron's been helping out. I think he's going to propose. He's a good man."

Ralph coughed as he inhaled too much of his cigarette.

"Byron? What is this, a Jane Austen novel? Tell that asshole to take his cashmere scarf and shove it up his ass."

"I'll hang up if you say those things."

Ralph hated when Sandra didn't react to his outbursts. It made him feel especially childish.

"What do you want me to say, that I'm okay Natters has some other man watching over her? I'm not, for the record. I never will be."

"Sure you aren't Ralph. I bet you're outside a bar smoking a cigarette. You'll forget about this call in a couple hours."

Ralph wanted to throw his phone against a wall. He couldn't believe how predictable he'd become.

"Do you want the money or not? I've been meaning to buy a new computer but not if I'm going to be accused of being a deadbeat."

"No, that's okay. You keep the money. Get a computer. Maybe enroll in some community college classes or something. Have you thought about life after clowning?"

Life after clowning? He most certainly had not. "Sandra, you should have seen me the other day. A Beverly Hills guy that saw the old Fuzzy and Jango show, back in the day, hired us to do a gig. I did part of my old act, you know, the juggling while riding the unicycle. Stayed on it while wearing clown shoes peddling on a goddamned lawn. Now, Manuel's talking about a reality show out in Texas that's looking for clowns and they're interested in me. I'm back. I'm going to be on television."

He kept the phone up to his ear as he took another drag. He didn't care if Sandra could hear him as long as he could absorb every bit of praise she'd undoubtedly have to give him.

"Us," she said. "You've got a new partner."

Rage filled him as he struggled to process how in the world that could've been the only thing that she'd taken away from all he'd said.

"That's the question you ask? No congratulations or anything? Well, for your information, she's not my partner.

She's my assistant when we're performing. Just a birthday party princess who attached herself to my little gig. We're making good money, though."

"You're fucking her aren't you?" Ralph shook his head in disbelief.

"What do you care?" he asked, trying not to sound too defensive.

"It's a matter of reality Ralph. Something you've always struggled to accept. You're not going to be on TV and you can't be a clown forever. You need to figure something out that's going to set you up for the future."

He'd almost had enough of her criticism. "I told you, I'm making good money. Things are good."

"Ralph, listen to me. This can't go on for the rest of your life. You may have had a good week, good couple weeks, I'm happy for you. You're getting on in years and you need to think about savings, retirement, and the whatever comes next. I know you don't have health care. You understand this?"

He knew she'd made some good points. It pained him to listen to what she had to say and not completely disagree. That didn't change one simple fact.

"What else am I going to do? This is it. I'm a clown. Maybe in more ways than one. I'm forty-six. There is no life after clowning for me. I'm nothing without Jango."

She didn't immediately respond. Ralph heard heavy breathing through the phone. She might even be crying.

"Look, dinner's almost ready. I've got to go. There are things out there for you. I read about North Dakota and Alaska. There's work to be had for people who know what hard work is. I know you know how to handle the grind. You know that, too. Just keep an open mind."

"Yea, you'd love that. Have me in the middle of fucking nowhere so you'd never have to worry about me seeing Natalie again. I see right through your shit Sandra. I'm not the only one who hasn't changed."

A few seconds passed. He thought she'd hung up, but then he heard, "Take care of yourself Ralph. I'll call you soon." The phone beeped and he found himself alone with his cigarette, wondering what the hell had just happened.

Part of him hated Sandra. She'd written off his accomplishments before she'd even stopped to consider the idea that he might have actually done something worthwhile. It made him reconsider whether or not he actually had.

One thing stuck out. She'd been right about his current path. It was unsustainable. He knew that. He also knew that doing something about it wouldn't be easy.

He knew Jules had to go. Her erratic behavior and total lack of respect for him would be the death of him. He could take it in small doses, but hearing about her throwing a brick through a windshield reminded him that she could bring his whole world crashing down in a matter of seconds.

He walked back into the Brimstone a changed man. For the past two weeks, he'd had something he'd been able to hold over Manuel. A sense of superiority isn't generally considered a positive trait, but Ralph liked being able to feel special for once in his life. Even if the girl he had was completely bat shit crazy.

Manuel perked up as he sat back down on his stool.

"Forgot to tell you, Barnyard Paul called. Said the producers for that show were hoping to look at some potential cast members next week or so. You down to go to Texas?"

"Sure," he said. "What else would I have to do?"

CHAPTER
Thirteen

IGNORING JULES TURNED OUT TO BE HARDER THAN RALPH expected. For all the negative traits that fit her like a pantsuit on a new aged millennial, stupidity wasn't one of them. She knew all the right buttons to push.

She texted him to pick her up to take her to the Brimstone Saloon the day after he'd had his call with Sandra. He managed to ignore that one, but Jules didn't know how to take a hint. Or, she just didn't want to.

His resiliency met its greatest match two days after that when she sent him a dirty picture of herself. Ralph never felt worse about himself than when he took the phone into the bathroom to pleasure himself, knowing that he could have the real thing with the simple push of a button.

She stayed with him, in his mind, wherever he went. He walked through CVS imagining himself eating her out down every aisle. At the grocery store, he pictured himself bent over while she shoved radishes up his ass after giving him a prune juice enema. Even when he tried to focus all his brainpower on something else, there was Jules, waiting to drag him on a leash back down the rabbit hole.

He sat waiting in the community college admissions office, thinking about how much sex students had on a daily basis. He wondered what kind of sex machine Jules would be if she'd attended university. She would have fit in well at clown school.

Worst of all, she interfered with his work. Right in the middle of balancing a bowling pin on his clown nose at a baptism party, he pictured Jules picking at her thong wedgie and the whole act came crumbling down to a chorus of boos. He'd made up for it by rummaging through the parents' bathroom cabinets for pill bottles but that didn't make him miss her any less.

A guidance counselor came out to greet him. "Ralph Touchet," a cheerful, elderly woman said. He nodded and walked into her office.

"What brings you to WCCC?" she asked. Ralph could think of no immediate response.

"Uh, to better myself I guess," he said, with an unintentionally inquisitive tone. The woman smiled.

"That's as good an answer as any. Why don't you tell me what you're good at?" she asked.

He paused again, trying to think of an answer besides the obvious one.

"I'm a clown," he replied. She sat up in her chair.

"That's okay. It takes some people longer than others to figure out where their talents lie. I'm sure you will someday. Why don't you tell me what your interests are instead?"

He cursed Sandra for planting this stupid and pointless

idea in his head.

"No, I'm a professional clown. You know, big red nose and lots of colorful clothing. It's what I do for a living."

The woman's face lit up.

"Oh, that's lovely. I didn't know those still existed. How wonderful."

Ralph couldn't help himself as he stood up. "Thank you for your time, but this isn't for me." He left without waiting for a response.

He thought of Fuzzy as he left the building. In a sick way, he envied his friend. Not for dying in a pumpkin patch, but for not having to grow old in a world that didn't have a place for elderly clowns. As morbid as it sounded, Fuzzy would always have a place in people's memories. Ralph didn't know where his place was anymore.

His phone vibrated. Jules. Common sense told him not to pick up. Ralph grew tired of listening to common sense.

"Go for Jango," he said as he picked up.

"Cute," Jules replied. Ralph didn't respond, regretting his decision to cave to his vulnerability.

"Look, I'm not oblivious to the fact that you've been ignoring me. I only called because I got a call from one of the parents at the Vasquez party requesting us both for their nephew's party tomorrow. I know it's last minute, but so do they and they've offered us three grand. That's the real number, too."

Ralph tried to detect any hint of dishonesty in her tone. She could very well be lying, but that didn't seem to matter.

"I see," he said.

"Well, I told you I wouldn't keep that shit from you

anymore. I also know that neither of us is in any position to turn that kind of money down. You in, or you out, clown?"

He missed hearing vintage Jules. Bitchy as she could be, her charm was near irresistible.

"All right," he said. "Text me the address princess. I'll see you there tomorrow." He hung up the phone before she could respond or demand a ride.

Ralph knew this could be a huge mistake. It didn't matter. Clowns don't run away from challenges. They juggle their way through the great maze of life, even if it means stepping on a couple rubber chickens along the way.

CHAPTER
Fourteen

ONE THOUGHT STUCK WITH RALPH AS HE VENTURED back to Beverly Hills. He was thankful that he didn't offer to give Jules a ride. Driving without a chain-smoking, prima donna allowed him to appreciate the scenery in a whole new light.

He arrived at the party an hour early, hoping that catering would have another meat platter. Dreaming of pigs in a blanket caused him to skip out on his own lunch, a hot dog on white bread. Unfortunately, he didn't see a catering van or an assistant with a headset as he approached the mansion.

A man came up to greet him as he pulled into the spacious driveway.

"Jango the Clown. I've heard a lot about you," said a balding asshole wearing khakis and a sports coat. Ralph shook his hand, saddened by the lack of an attractive assistant.

"Your partner arrived already. She's outside by the

bouncy castle. The kids are finishing up a movie in the downstairs theatre. You've got plenty of time to set up. Can I get you anything? Bottled water, energy bar? My name's Levi, by the way."

"Soft shell crab," Ralph replied, in a meek tone before he could stop himself.

"Pardon?" Levi asked.

"Never mind," Ralph said, as he walked toward the back of the house, saddened by the absence of crustaceans.

He spotted Jules, in her pink dress, sitting under an umbrella in typical, princess fashion. She watched him as he approached the table, but she didn't say anything. The two looked at each other for a few minutes, each unwilling to address the other. The sun beat down as the two performers endured their standstill. Ralph craved a cigarette, anything to take his mind off the person right in front of him.

Jules spoke first. "Well. Are you going to tell me what's been up your ass all week instead of my dildo?" Ralph chose not to respond.

"That's it then," she added. "You're not going to say anything? We fuck like rabbits until you suddenly go all rogue and you won't even say why. I knew a clown wouldn't be able to keep up."

"This is why I needed to get away from you. You're toxic, Jules. You wreck everything you touch and you make people feel horrible about themselves."

She pulled out a cigarette and stuck it in her mouth. "You know you really shouldn't smoke that out here," Ralph added. She lit it with one hand, giving him the finger with the other.

"You can't see it, can you clown? You know, I actually liked you. Thought you were someone I could actually be with. Guess I was wrong."

Ralph paced around the lawn, furious at her attempts to manipulate him.

"Can't you see things from my perspective? Why would I ever want to be with you after the way you treated me constantly? Can you name a single good reason?"

She blew smoke in his direction.

"Yes."

Ralph couldn't help but smack himself on the head, completely unsurprised by her answer. "I'm listening."

"Who else is going to want to be with you?" He took his clown nose off and threw it on the ground.

"This is exactly what I'm talking about. You're poison. Pure poison. You live for being cruel and making people feel worse about themselves than you do about yourself. You're rotten."

She stood up from her chair and stepped into the sunlight.

"Okay," she replied.

Ralph tried to see through her bullshit. He couldn't figure out what angle she was trying to play.

"That's not a real answer. That's just you deflecting because you don't want to face the truth. You're a horrible person. That is why I've been ignoring you. I've seen the light."

She laughed.

"You think that's funny," Ralph said.

"No, I think you're funny," Jules replied, as she blew a smoke ring.

Ralph threw up his arms.

"I can't do this. I don't care how good the money is. It's not worth it. I'm leaving."

He started to walk away, completely at peace with his decision to forego fifteen hundred dollars. He thought about going to the Brimstone when he heard her say, "You want the truth?"

He wanted his foot to move forward. He couldn't help but turn around. If this was the last time he'd ever see Jules, he wanted to at least hear her out properly.

"Yea," he said. "Tell me the truth. That is, your truth." He crossed his arms in an attempt to show that he meant business.

"Here's how I see it, clown. Neither one of us is ever going to be anything. You can try to deny it, but we both know it's true. We're performers. We're nothing. We're never going to be anything more than that and in a few years, no one is going to hire either one of us. So we can go our separate ways and take life as it takes us, up the ass with hot sauce lube, or we can face our grim futures together. I'm a horrible person and you're one ugly motherfucker. A perfect fit if I've ever seen one."

He let her words soak in for a moment. She didn't pull any punches, but she hadn't said anything untrue either. He had a decision to make.

Images of people from his past cluttered his mind as he stared at his Jules, his princess. He saw Fuzzy, Sandra, and Natalie, people he loved, people he left, people who no longer needed him. He could choose to believe that there was some chance his daughter would want him to be a regular fixture of her life and that he had the ability to make that happen. A nice dream, but one that would never become a reality.

Ralph thought about how much he'd fucked up his past. Things he couldn't change. A world that didn't have a place for him.

"You're right," he said. "We are perfect for each other." He saw her familiar smile return through the smoke.

"Good. Very good. You ever fucked on a bouncy castle?"

Nothing about Jules surprised him anymore.

"No," he said. Jules opened her mouth to say something, but Ralph cut her off. "But I'd like to."

He gave the house a quick look. The windows were devoid of faces that might catch them in the lewd act of public sexual intercourse. He nodded at Jules as she climbed through the netting into the inflatable palace.

Ralph spotted something in the grass as he kicked off his shoes. He picked up his clown nose and put it where it belonged.

"Come on, clown," Jules called. He ignored the sign on the castle entrance that told him to remove his oversized footwear and climbed inside.

The bouncy castle swayed back and forth as Ralph did his best to keep his composure. He thought of the unicycle, which had a similar level of instability. This did him little good, as he fell flat on his face next to Jules.

"Adorable," she said. "Now do me from behind. Let's

hope this works out better than the last time."

Ralph paused to make sure he'd heard her correctly. "You remember Del Taco?" he asked.

"Of course I do, Cousin Bark's shit never works."

Though he couldn't understand what was going on as he found himself oddly aroused. Jules remembered a disgusting event that would cause any sane person to cut off all contact with the person they'd experienced it with. Ralph couldn't exactly define the foreign emotion that took control of his entire being, but if he had to guess, he'd call it love.

He put one hand on Jules back and lifted up her skirts with the other. He reached deep into her gown and used both hands to pull down her underwear. In one fluid motion, he removed his suspenders and pulled his trousers down to his feet.

Nothing felt more natural as Ralph kneeled behind his princess, inserting himself into her like water on a Chia Pet. He forgot his sad existence as he thrust everything he had into the one woman who dared to call him a companion. The ground quaked and trembled like a Lean Cuisine that had been left in the microwave for too long.

Jules screamed with pleasure that sounded like a woman who'd successfully navigated a Filene's Basement flash sale. Her shrieks of pleasure motivated him to up his tempo, moving faster than VHS tape in a rewinding machine. Nothing could get in their way, nothing except a voice.

"What's the noise? Where'd they go?" Ralph stumbled as he tried to pull his pants up. He stepped up in the bouncy castle and tripped, falling out the entrance. He hit the grass with a loud thump, though thankfully his pants stayed around his waist, preventing him from exposing himself to the partygoers.

A woman screamed. "Those sick freaks. Levi, call the police. Somebody, stop them." Ralph checked to make sure his clown nose was still on his face. He took a brief glance at the house and then turned to the bouncy castle again.

"Jules, I think you need to come out here. Now." He held the entrance opened as she tried her best to exit the inflatable fortress.

Ralph looked around. He saw faces looking at them from the windows. The party was definitely not going to happen. There was only one thing left to do.

"We need to run," he said. She looked over at her heels near the table.

"I need my shoes," she said.

"Leave them," Ralph replied, as he grabbed her hand. The two began to sprint across the lawn at an impressive speed for smokers in their mid-forties.

Ralph smiled as they made their way across the grounds. Faced with danger, he saw life from a different perspective. He could understand why Jules acted the way she did. Doing bad things was very entertaining.

"Somebody stop them," the woman yelled. Ralph didn't turn back to see if anyone obeyed the woman's command.

"Faster Jules," he called, as he pulled her forward.

They reached his truck. He pulled out his keys as he spotted Levi approaching. Jules climbed inside and Ralph tossed her the keys. He hesitated with his hand on the door for a second.

"Stop right there you sick fuck. I'm not going to let either of you get away with this." Levi had his fists up as he moved toward the truck.

Ralph walked toward the man attempting to impede their escape.

"Did anyone ever tell you the story of the man who got in the clown's way? I'll tell you what Levi, it's really fucking funny."

He pulled one of his rubber balls out from a pocket and threw it at Levi, hitting him in the head. Levi's fists trembled with fear as he ran away screaming for his wife. Ralph quickly retrieved his prize possession and climbed into his truck. He put it in gear and floored it right through the gate.

Once they reached the main road, Jules asked, "Where are we going, clown?" She lit a cigarette and handed it to him. Ralph took a long puff, allowing himself to fully appreciate the adrenaline rush.

"Texas," he replied. "I've got to see a man about a rodeo."

ACKNOWLEDGEMENTS

I'd like to especially thank Jessica Baumgartner for her help on this project.

I'd also like to both thank and apologize to my mother for reading this book. An idea is a terrible thing to waste!

To switch things up in the acknowledgements section, which look rather similar from book to book, I'd like to thank a few of my grad school friends who listened to various readings as this was being written. Cody Diliberto, Ashley Call, and especially to Wendy Martin, whose class subconsciously inspired Ralph's last name.

Other family & friends, I thank you. Please continue to buy my books or I'll stop including this bit in the acknowledgements.

Finally, to you the readers, I thank you. We've been through many genres together. Your support, compliments, and friendship continue to inspire me. Namaste.

OTHER BOOKS BY IAN
Thomas Malone

A Trip Down Reality Lane

Courting Mrs. McCarthy

THE DIALOGUES

Five College Dialogues

Five More College Dialogues

Five High School Dialogues

Dead Batteries Tell No Tales:
A Prequel to Five High School Dialogues